LOVE

and Other
Four-Letter Words

LOVE

and Other
Four-Letter Words

·CAROLYN·
·MACKLER·

DELACORTE PRESS

Published by
Delacorte Press
an imprint of
Random House Children's Books
a division of Random House, Inc.
1540 Broadway
New York, New York 10036

Visit us on the Web! www.randomhouse.com/teens
Educators and librarians, for a variety of teaching tools, visit us at
www.randomhouse.com/teachers

Library of Congress Cataloging-in-Publication Data
Mackler, Carolyn.
　　Love and other four-letter words / by Carolyn Mackler.
　　　　p. cm.
　　Summary: When she and her mother move to an apartment in New York City
after her parents decide on a trial separation, sixteen-year-old Sammie learns to
deal with her mother's fragile mental state, her best friend's self-centeredness,
several new friendships, and her own budding sexuality.
　　ISBN 0-385-32743-9
　　[1. Interpersonal relations—Fiction.　　2. Family problems—Fiction.
3. Self-perception—Fiction.]　I. Title.
PZ7.M2178 Lo 2000
[Fic]—dc21　　　　　　　　　　　　　　　　　　　00-025189

The text of this book is set in 12.25-point Berkeley Book.
Book design by Alyssa Morris

Manufactured in the United States of America
October 2000
10 9 8 7 6 5 4 3 2 1
BVG

To my parents, Anne Dalton and Ian Mackler,
for believing in me

Acknowledgments

MANY THANKS to Amy Berkower and Jodi Reamer at Writers House and Beverly Horowitz at Random House Children's Books; my editor, Françoise Bui, always with a keen eye and a pencil in hand; Judy Blume and Paula Danziger, for inspiring me and then becoming real people.

Also, to my extended clan of family and friends, for reading, rereading, listening and discussing. Special thanks to Alison and Michelle, my beloved stepsisters and ever-ready teen focus group.

CHAPTER ONE

Let's say someone had waltzed up to me six months ago and asked for my definition of love. I wasn't so naïve at fifteen and a half to presume that love, or *luv*—as my best friend, Kitty, always ends her e-mails—only applies to sex-crazed teenagers, pressed against lockers, feverishly grinding groins in between classes. I'd probably have rambled on about the bond between mothers and fathers, parents and children. No doubt I would have sprinkled in choice phrases like "unconditional support," "mutual respect," and "considering the other person's feelings."

Pull me aside now and quiz me about those same four letters, and I'd blankly stare at you, my jaw ajar, like those guys who sat behind me in biology all year.

Kitty would say I'm jaded. I would say that's a major understatement, seeing how my entire life has been blown to smithereens. Unconditional support has gone the way of the pterodactyl. Mutual respect? Only exists in the pages of the self-help books on Mom's bedside table. And my feelings definitely weren't being considered when Dad dropped the bombshell on that Sunday afternoon in early May.

I'd just returned from sleeping over at Kitty's, where we pulled an all-nighter because her boyfriend, Jack, called from his cell phone at three A.M. to report that he and two friends were on her back porch. Kitty had answered on the second ring, before her parents woke up, so we slipped into sweats and sneaked out the sliding glass doors. They were all wasted; I could smell it on their breath. And moments after Kitty and Jack disappeared into the pool shed, both guys conked out on reclining chairs, a gesture I tried not to take personally. I almost crept back to Kitty's room, but then I remembered an article I once read about an inebriated frat boy choking to death on his own puke. So I held a vigil until pinkish light accented the sky and the *luv*ers reappeared on the deck: Jack's T-shirt inside out, three nickel-sized hickeys dotting Kitty's neck.

By the time I got home the next afternoon, my eyelids were drooping and my throat felt scratchy and dry. All I wanted to do was take a hot shower and burrow under my covers, but an eerie stillness permeated the house.

"Mom's in bed with a migraine," Dad reported in a hushed tone, pressing his outstretched pointer finger against his lips, steering me into the family room for A Discussion.

As I perched on the edge of our leather recliner, I tugged at the frayed strings on my cutoff jean shorts. Upon retrieving them from a bottom drawer on Friday afternoon, I'd discovered to my displeasure that they were snugger than last summer.

"Sammie." He paused. "Mom and I have been talking a lot these past few weeks. . . ."

Dad's voice trailed off. I noticed that the creases that have been cutting into his cheeks all spring were obscured by a weekend's buildup of stubble.

". . . And we've decided to get a trial separation."

Trial separation. The term hung in the air between us, like humidity before a thunderstorm. I began wrapping a thread from my shorts around my finger.

"What about our plan to go to California next year?" I asked. Dad is an English professor at Cornell, and Mom and I were joining him on his sabbatical to Stanford at the end of June. Aunt Jayne, Dad's younger sister, just sent a photo of the half-of-a-house she'd found for us in Palo Alto.

Dad began gnawing his fingernails, a habit he kicked five years ago, in solidarity with Mom, who was becoming a vegetarian because of her high cholesterol.

After a long silence, Dad somberly replied, "I'm going out there alone after all."

My face froze. *Alone?* Maybe he means alone, as in alone *without* Mom, as in alone *with* me. That had to be it. It's no secret that Dad and I are close, much closer than I am to Mom.

If the trial separation announcement was an atomic bomb, an obliteration of the belief that Mom and Dad were the *7th Heaven*, we-have-problems-yet-we-gleefully-work-them-through type of parents, what was about to come was nuclear devastation. Armageddon. To quote that REM song, "the end of the world as we know it."

Dad got up from the couch, affixed his arm around my shoulders and delivered the final blow: "I'm sorry . . . it's just something I have to do."

I was stunned. Utterly, completely stunned. So stunned I couldn't speak, even though I was aching to scream, to rant, to demand an explanation for how he could desert me like this. All I could do was repeat, over and over in my head: *Don't feel a thing. Don't feel a thing. Don't feel a thing.*

It was only as I wriggled away from Dad's arm that I noticed my finger was red and bulging. I'd twisted the thread so tightly it had cut off the circulation. Yet still, as I unwound the tourniquet to discover purplish grooves in my skin, I didn't feel a thing.

✦ ✦ ✦

There was this time last summer when Kitty and I rode our bikes all over Ithaca, ending up at Stewart Park. As we unlaced our sneakers and waded into Cayuga Lake, a motorboat whipped by, towing a small boy on an oversized yellow inner tube. The kid, both hands gripping the plastic handles, had a frantic expression on his face as his pleas to stop were swallowed by the rumble of the horsepower. The spotter was consumed with smearing on sunblock, the driver consumed with two bikini-clad women capsizing a Sunfish. Which left the boy two options: to catapult himself into murky waters, or to get dragged along, completely out of his control, until the powers-that-be decided to terminate his joyride. He chose the latter.

I kept revisiting that image over the next few weeks, as I watched my life being disassembled, one familiarity at a time. I avoided Dad assiduously until his late-May departure, as soon as Cornell let out. And I only talked to Mom when absolutely necessary. Like when the conversation swung to the looming question at hand: next year.

Mom had already taken a leave of absence from her job as an art teacher at the middle school. And in a matter of weeks, a faceless family who'd agreed to sublet from us back in February would be pulling into the driveway, stocking the cupboards, peeing in the toilets of the home I've lived in since I was two years old. This is all I know about them, from the realtor's letter that lay open on Mom's dresser:

1. The man's name is Dr. Oscar Mueller.
2. He's going to teach statistics at Cornell and his wife will work at the vet school.
3. They're from Cincinnati.
4. They have one teenager.

Because of the father's name, I call them the Oscar Mayer Wieners. The worst part is knowing that the kid is going to curl up in my bed. Especially if it happens to be a boy, in light of what I recently read on this "let's-get-teens-to-chat-about-sex" Web site:

I'm a fifteen-year old guy, joeshmoe wrote, *and I spank the monkey once a day, my morning ritual.*

That's it? responded pistol99. *I jerk off more frequently than dentists brush their teeth.*

Whenever I think about Oscar Mayer Wienerboy whacking away on my mattress, I feel a pulsing between my legs. I didn't tell anyone *that*, but I did describe to Kitty how, probably because he's from Ohio, I picture him to have moppy golden hair, freckles, and a blade of grass in the corner of his mouth. Which Kitty said was preposterous, because, to the best of her knowledge, there are no farms in Cincinnati.

I suggested to Mom that we rent a town house in Fairview Heights for the year, until the Oscar Mayer Wieners clear out. When I was in fifth grade, my friend Shelly and her mother moved there after her father ran off with an undergrad. It doesn't take a psychotherapist to recognize that after the trauma of a separation, the best thing we could do was to keep everything else in our lives as stable as possible.

But that's when Mom started up about New York City, where she lived two decades ago, when she met Dad. And then, a few weeks later, she signed a lease for a one-bedroom apartment on the Upper West Side.

"That translates to uptown and west of Central Park," she chirped as she popped a strawberry in her mouth. She'd just returned from the five-hour drive and was sitting at the kitchen table, thumbing through *Feel the Fear and Do It Anyway.*

"Whatever that means." I shrugged.

Mom peered at me over the rim of her reading glasses. I was tempted to add that the title of her book should be changed to *Ignore Your Daughter and Do It Anyway*. But I didn't. Instead I grabbed a strawberry out of the pint, rinsed it in the sink and started upstairs, my throat tightening, making it difficult to catch my breath.

That's been happening a lot in the past month, these breathing attacks, like a fist strangling my neck, transforming a simple inhale into a task as huge as scaling Mount Kilimanjaro. No matter how much I yawn or stretch my arms in front of me, all I get are shallow gasps that make my chest ache.

It happens whenever I think about Dad. How I barely say anything when he calls, just *fine* this and *fine* that and *do you want me to put Mom on now?* How I locked myself in my room and blasted my CDs that morning Mom drove him to the Syracuse airport. How I gnawed the inside of my cheeks until they were raw as he pounded on my door and eventually called to Mom: *I don't know what to do, Roz . . . I'm going to miss my plane.* I couldn't make out Mom's response, but the knocking stopped soon after.

"Life's a car ride," Kitty said when I described my decaying home life. Ever since she got her license everything is a driving metaphor. "Sometimes it's cruise control down smooth highways . . . other times it's potholes on rural roads."

"Yeah, well, I forgot to pack my motion sickness bag," I snorted.

I know just how Mom would react if she heard that.

You're being melodramatic, she would say, swatting the air with her palm. Well, Mom's one to talk, seeing how she's a regular emotional roller coaster. Typical for an artist or a Cancer, of which she is both. Mom thrives on change, constantly seeking new tastes, new landscapes, new routes to the grocery store. When Mom is on a peak, I wish she came equipped with a volume knob, so I could turn her down. But land her in a valley and it's tears, headaches, hives, you name it. When she was little, her older brother nicknamed her Onion because she cried so much.

I'm exactly the opposite, like Dad. We're much more even-keeled. We'd opt for our favorite pasta place rather than the Thai-Cuban-Scandinavian restaurant that just opened downtown. And Dad used to joke that Mom emoted enough for the three of us. I guess that's one way to put the fact that we keep a lot to ourselves. We don't let the entire population see every emotion we're feeling every second that we're feeling it.

I didn't even cry when Mom returned from the airport and locked herself in the upstairs bathroom with the tub running. Or when she emerged, eyes bloodshot, and asked what I wanted for my birthday, which was three days later. All I said was: *For none of this to be happening.*

It's not like I expected turning sixteen to be Hollywood-esque, with a shiny new car in the driveway and a boyfriend at my side. I haven't even gotten my learner's permit yet, and the closest I've come to romance is a guy I kissed at sailing camp last summer. I didn't even like him that much, but Kitty thought I should do it, for the experience. After all, more than one hand had groped inside her bra, and a goalie from the soccer camp across the road was hinting around her shorts.

Just open your mouth and pretend you're writing the alphabet with your tongue, Kitty coached.

Well, I barely got to E before he began pressing the hard bulge in his swimsuit against my right thigh. And the kiss was so slobbery, the first thing I did when I got back to the bunk was chug a gallon of Scope.

So I knew better than to expect sixteen to be the time of my life, but I never imagined it would be like this. Whoever coined "*sweet* sixteen" must have had some Norman Rockwell delusion of poodle-skirted girls rocking around the clock with boys who used words like *swell*. All before their nine o'clock curfew, of course.

C H A P T E R

T W O

So that's why, barely seven hours after I finished my biology Regents, when I should have been celebrating the end of tenth grade, I was dividing my worldly possessions into piles to bring, piles to store in the garage and piles of maybes, unfortunately the biggest pile of all.

It's not like I forfeited these fantastic plans to stay home tonight. Kitty and I usually spend the last day of school renting movies and bingeing on frozen yogurt, but she and Jack were headed to some party. Even if I didn't have to pack, I doubt I would have joined them. Jack, who's a forward on the varsity basketball team, runs with the Beautiful People. It's not as if Jack himself is that beautiful—his face is sort of mashed in, like he smacked into a brick wall at a high speed—but being a Beautiful Person is not so much about looks as attitude. I should know. During the handful of parties Jack has taken us to, I've had an abundance of time to record mental notes because, other than minor details, they all went exactly like this:

1. We arrive. I suddenly remember that after the last party, I vowed never to attend another as long as I live.
2. Jack gets swept up in a flurry of high fives and back slaps. Kitty, surgically attached to his J. Crew shirt, disappears into a cloud of cigarette smoke.
3. I scan for familiar faces, maybe receive a limp wave from the girl who scammed answers off me in geometry last week. Someone hands me a warm beer in an oversized plastic cup. I sip slowly, hating the taste of beer but wondering if a slight buzz could transform me into the life of the party. Very doubtful. Search for a dark corner.
4. Eventually found by Kitty, who is distraught and in desperate need of counsel because:
   a. some bitch is flirting with Jack, and while he's not reciprocating he's also not ignoring.
   OR

b. Jack is flirting with some bitch. Well, not flirting exactly, but he just asked her if she was on the cover of last month's *Cosmo*.

5. Once Kitty flits off to find Jack again, I consider why no one of the male gender is entering my dark corner of the world. Wonder if I'm:

a. sexually repulsive.

b. in deficiency of pheromones, which is this scent that animals emit to attract a mate.

c. invisible.

6. We leave by midnight. I vow never to attend another party as long as I live.

✦ ✦ ✦

By ten P.M., the radio was tuned to WICB, the Station for Innovation, and I was loading my books into a cardboard box. Mom had said it would be fine to stack them on the top shelves, but the last thing I wanted was to have the Oscar Mayer Wieners snooping through my personal belongings. Especially if they came across the racy Harlequin Romances that Kitty gave me in seventh grade, key sections highlighted.

I must have been in my own world because the next thing I knew, Mom was standing in the doorway, wearing paint-splattered overalls with a lacy black camisole underneath. A paisley bandanna was holding back her long blackish hair.

"Thanks for knocking." My door had been closed, but not locked, because it's an iron rule in our house to do the standard three-rap before you enter a room.

"I was . . . for about ten minutes. You've got to turn down that music, Sammie. I can barely hear myself think."

My full name is Samantha Leigh Davis, but ever since I was a baby everyone has called me Sammie. Several times, I've asked my parents if it was their idea of a joke to give their only child the same name as Sammy Davis, Jr., one of the ensemble of 1950s entertainers called the Rat Pack.

We named you after Mom's father, Samuel, who died when she was thirteen, Dad usually says.

And, frankly, Mom always adds, *Sammy Davis, Jr., didn't dawn on us when we started calling you Sammie.*

Didn't dawn on her! Just like it's not dawning on her now to give me more than a millisecond to get to my stereo? Before I'd been able to set down my armful of paperbacks, Mom tromped across the room and lowered the volume to a barely audible pitch.

"You could've let me turn it down myself," I said.

"Don't use that tone of voice with me."

Tone of voice is a biggie in Mom's lexicon. I admit, I

wouldn't have won any Pollyanna awards recently. But these last few weeks, Mom's been so sensitive that if I allow the faintest hint of emotion to enter my voice, she careens across the room.

I folded my arms across my chest and faced Mom. We stared at each other for a few seconds, like gunslingers in an Old West showdown. That's when I noticed the purple half circles under her eyes. Without them, Mom would look about twenty-five, not forty-two, which she actually is. Every once in a while, people ask if we're sisters. I never know if they're being sincere, because we don't look that much alike, except we're both around five feet five and have brown eyes. I wish I'd gotten Dad's eyes, which are hazel with rusty flecks that appear almost orange if he wears a certain color shirt.

I did inherit Dad's straight brown hair, which I've kept right below my shoulders for practically my whole life. There's nothing else to do with it. For a while, in junior high, I attempted styling it with various products pawned off on me by overly optimistic hairdressers. But it never made a difference, except to make me look like I'd had a run-in with a jar of rubber cement. Eventually I gave up and resigned myself to my fate: to be absolutely, completely average.

Mom finally broke the silence.

"Look, I'm driving down to the A&P to get more boxes," she said. "I just wanted to see if you'd like anything."

"I don't think you could get what I want at the A&P."

Mom ignored that comment. "Some Ben & Jerry's or a Frozfruit?"

I shook my head. A lump was lodging in my esophagus.

"The more you resist this change, the harder it's going to be," Mom said.

I didn't want her to see that I was struggling to catch my breath, so I turned toward my bookshelf and surveyed the stack of remaining paperbacks. I wasn't in the mood for homilies tonight.

" 'Time moves like a river,' " Mom continued, quoting the John Stewart song Dad used to listen to when he was feeling melancholy, " 'you can either sink or swim.' "

And that's what got me. I pivoted around, sucking in a pathetic gasp of air. "Please tell me the next time you're giving an inspirational seminar, because I'll remember to sign up."

"Have it your way," Mom snapped, starting down the hallway. But when she reached the stairs, she spun on her heel. "Just make sure you finish your room. The movers are coming at noon and anything we don't send with them gets stored in the garage."

I almost yelled back, *What does it look like I'm doing?* But instead I reached over and blasted the volume on my stereo again.

People think it's strange when I tell them I am closer to Dad than Mom, as if the only things fathers are good for are briefing you on current events or lubing your bike chain. It's not even that Dad and I chat the way I do with Kitty, it's more that we like to do the same things. Or I guess I should say *liked.* Up until last month we were always planning hikes or cycling into the farmland surrounding Ithaca. And ever since Christmas, when Dad gave me his old guitar from college, he'd been teaching me chords to folk songs. Kitty always teases me that I'm a hippie-chick, which I don't even think is such a bad thing after all.

Sometimes I wonder if Mom resented our bond, if she felt like the odd person out in the Davis clan. *Resentment.* That's what Mom and Dad's last blowout was about, back in April, when they returned from a dinner party hosted by the dean of the Arts School. I'd gone up to bed already, so I'd only caught this sound bite:

Mom: *I can't stand the way everyone looks down their*

noses at me, as if I show kids how to glue Popsicle sticks into birdcages for a living.

Dad: *Don't harbor resentment against Cornell for the way your life hasn't turned out, Roz . . . or against me, for that matter.*

Mom: *Well, if it weren't for Cornell, or you, for that matter, I wouldn't be stuck in this godforsaken town.*

I'd be the first to agree that Mom doesn't mesh with Ithaca. Take last year's holiday chorus recital. All the other parents wore jeans and coats, with the occasional red and green sweater. But Mom arrived in a purple velvet cape and glittery silver leggings that hugged her curvaceous hips. I'd gotten an earlier ride from the soprano who lives two doors down, so I almost keeled over when I spotted her. And then, during the final number, they invited the audience to join in on "Let There Be Peace on Earth." Instead of mouthing the words like all the other parents, Mom let her voice echo through the auditorium (*And let it begin with meeeeee . . .*) so loudly I wanted to crawl under the risers.

I guess that's the biggest difference between Mom and me. Where I'm more at ease being a chameleon, Mom thinks idiosyncrasies are what make a person interesting. At least that's what she said on the first day of eighth grade, when I wound up in her art class.

Rule #1, she'd scribbled on the chalkboard: *Call me Roz. Mrs. Davis is my mother-in-law.* Once the initial astonishment had rippled through the classroom, she'd selected a fresh piece of phlegm-colored chalk and written, *Rule #2: The only rule in art is that there are no rules.*

After the bell rang, as we were filing into the hallway, a chorus of classmates fed me that *your-mom-is-so-cool-I-bet-you-can-get-away-with-murder* line. I just shrugged and shifted my notebooks onto my hip. I didn't tell them about the day before, when I'd returned from Buttermilk Falls only to hear the Doors reverberating through the cul-de-sac, originating from our house. Nor did I say how uneasy it had made me to discover Mom grooving around the family room to "Light My Fire," shaking her boobs as if she were some Vegas showgirl. Nor did I say that since I wasn't forecasting homicide in my future, all I wanted was a garden-variety mom like Kitty's. Mrs. Lundquist lived in freshly pressed blouses and slacks, muted tones only, and was constantly dashing out to town board meetings.

As I dragged a box of books over to the doorway, I switched on my fan. It was warm and muggy out, a typical central New York early-summer night. Even though my windows were open, there wasn't the slightest hint of a breeze. The elastic from my bra felt sticky against my skin. I reached under my T-shirt, unhooked the back, slipped an arm through the strap and pulled my bra out the other sleeve.

There's something I *did* inherit from Mom: big breasts. Not gigantic, but enough so they sag without an underwire bra. Enough so some jerk in gym class last year called me Grand Tetons, after those mountains in Wyoming. Enough so they make me appear heavier than I actually am. And I'm not even heavy, though next to Kitty, who is four inches taller and fourteen pounds lighter than me, I must look like a whale.

Curvy is what I'd call myself on a good day. On a bad day, I try not to look in the mirror. I'm probably about as insecure as the next girl, which is to say that I wish my thighs didn't splay out when I sit down or my stomach didn't look pregnant after a second helping. Or I could lose those awful, pinkish stretch marks that recently appeared on my hips. My pediatrician suggested vitamin E oil, which I rubbed on them religiously for two weeks. But then I missed a day, a week, and eventually I gave up altogether.

I should know better than to compare myself to Kitty. Besides the tall thing and the skinny thing and the blond thing, there's the guy thing. Even though she's been going out with Jack for five months, she's still a natural-born flirt. Like she knows exactly how to shake her hips or twitter at guys' jokes, even if she's already heard them. I could never pull the giggling number off. I'd probably wind up sounding like a hyena with rabies. Besides, I'm well aware that guys didn't frequent our table in the snack bar because of *me*. It sounds awful, but if you saw a Jaguar and a Ford Taurus parked next to each other, which one would *you* want to drive?

The other thing about Kitty is that she's really smart. Like she and her parents are planning a road trip to Harvard and Yale this fall. Like we can cram for a test together and she'll ace it, bonus question included, and I'll walk away with a B-plus. *Exemplary* is how teachers always describe her. Just like they say I'm a *team player,* which I hate. Because I suck at organized sports, and anyway, it's just a euphemism for absolutely, completely average. Which is why I've always felt lucky someone like Kitty wants me for a best friend.

We met on the first day of third grade, when some boys on the playground were meowing at her, making fun of her name. She began to cry, not out loud, just little tears slipping down her pale cheeks. To this day it beats me how I mustered the courage to march over and say, *She's not crying . . . it's just allergies.* And then I led her to a shady spot under the poplar trees and offered her a crumpled tissue that had been in my pocket, making sure to tell her it was still clean.

That's when she told me that her real name is Katarina Lundquist. And that her father is Swedish, so she's bilingual, which sounded like the pasta dish I'd ordered at dinner the night before. And that her American mother met her father in Stockholm on her junior year abroad. It all sounded so exotic, especially since my parents got married at City Hall and don't even have photographs to show for it.

And we've been Best Friends Forever since then. At least that's what we carved into a poplar tree on the last day of third grade, after deciding that the blood sister thing was passé, what with the AIDS epidemic. Kitty's father is a physician, so she was the one to point that out. Because up until that moment, AIDS had never crossed my mind, except as this thing school nurses warned us about, for when we got older. But by junior high, I'd written more than one paper on the HIV virus. And by high school, the PTA and school board were having scathing debates about handing out condoms in school, whether it was a means to prevent STDs or a green light for kids to have sex.

It was also by high school that Kitty started acting sophisticated on me. Suddenly she was hyperconscious about how she appeared, clucking her tongue if I so much as cracked up in public. I think it has to do with wanting to be a Beautiful Person, which is absurd because we used to mutually disdain them as shallower than a wading pool. But when I reminded her of that, she accused me of putting up a defensive front, rejecting them before they could reject me.

Let's just say I do that, I considered saying. *Have they ever given me reason not to?*

In global studies a few weeks ago, Mr. Rizzoli drew a long horizontal line on the chalkboard, to illustrate the political spectrum. On the far left he wrote "radical" and explained that radicals are people who do things like strap themselves to redwoods to protest the lumber industry. Just left of center, he scribbled "liberal"; right of center, "conservative." And then, way off to the far right, he wrote "reactionary." *Reactionaries are people who want to return to the way things used to be,* he said.

Then he gave us an assignment to detail three reasons for why we are where we are on the spectrum. For a split second I thought about writing an essay entitled "Why I Am an Emotional Reactionary." Because the truth is, I wouldn't mind winding the clock back a few years. Back to when I could guess what would happen on the next page of my life. Back to when things with Kitty were less complicated. Back to when Mom and Dad were a rock-solid institution. But, of course, I didn't. Instead, I declared myself a liberal, citing abortion, the death penalty and tax cuts, just like everyone else in the class.

CHAPTER THREE

I was fast asleep when the phone rang the next morning. The sun had been glaring into my window since about five-thirty, when I'd wriggled out of my damp cotton nightgown and buried my head under a pillow to drown out the blue jays. I'd had a hard time falling asleep last night even though I was so exhausted I thought I'd conk out the second I closed my eyes. Instead I'd lain there thinking, *This is it. The last night in my room. As of tomorrow it's a pullout futon in the living room of a dinky apartment, with Mom a few steps away.* And it was like I'd downed a double shot of espresso.

The phone kept ringing. Mom must have already disconnected the answering machine. Where was she, anyway? The last I'd seen of her was in the middle of the night, when I'd heard a crash from the hallway. I'd stumbled out of bed and cracked open my door. Shielding my eyes from the light, I'd glimpsed Mom, surrounded by a swirl of towels, picture frames and cardboard boxes. Even though her back was to me, I could have sworn she was sobbing.

After the millionth ring, I wrapped myself in my sheet and dashed down the hall. Clearing my throat, I lifted the cordless to my ear.

"Hello?" I asked as I sank onto the bed. Mom had already stripped off her bedding, so the mattress scratched against my bare skin. I rearranged the sheet so it was under my thighs.

"Sammie? Are you up yet?"

I groaned and rubbed my eyes. That's another thing about Kitty. She tends to forget that the only other humans who rise as early as she does are bakers and dairy farmers.

"Now I am," I said, eyeing the book sprawled on the floor next to Mom's bed. The purple cover of *You Can Heal Your Life* was adorned with a brigade of boldly sketched hearts, three of which were pregnant with one-line affirmations. Something about the scrawled messages—*I am at Peace, I Love Myself, All is Well*—made me feel queasy.

"I just got back from running," Kitty said. "I didn't want to miss you before you left."

"What time is it?"

"A little before eight. Do you want to meet at Lincoln Street Diner around eight-thirty for a quick breakfast?"

I suddenly had to pee really badly. I wedged the phone between my ear and shoulder and headed into the bathroom off the master bedroom.

"If you bike down, I'll drive you home."

"Eight-forty-five?" I lifted the toilet seat lid and sat down.

"Okay. That'll give me time to take a shower." She paused. "And, Sammie?"

"Yeah?"

"Hope you had a nice pee."

I waited until we'd hung up before I flushed.

✦ ✦ ✦

I finally found Mom in the garage, duct-taping card-board boxes and labeling them with a black marker. She was wearing the same overalls as yesterday, which made me wonder if she'd even gone to bed. Her hair was pinned on top of her head in a tortoiseshell clip, but judging from the sweaty strands that clung to the back of her neck, it didn't look like she'd taken a shower.

Our chocolate Lab, Moxie, was sprawled on the ground, gnawing a ratty hunk of rawhide. Moxie wagged her tail as I dragged the stepladder over to where the bikes were hanging from a high hook. Mom frowned.

"I'm just going to meet Kitty for breakfast." I attempted to release my bike as quickly as possible. "I'll be back in an hour."

"One hour," Mom repeated, glancing at her watch.

A few minutes later, I was pedaling through Cayuga Heights on my burnt-orange Trek Hybrid, aka Mariposa. That means "butterfly" in Spanish, the language I started taking freshman year. It's halfway between a mountain bike and a touring bike, and one of my most treasured possessions, along with my guitar. I'm going to miss Mariposa in New York City, but Mom was firm that she remain in Ithaca: no room, not safe, will not budge.

It's not like I'm this star athlete or anything. I mean, I wouldn't know what to do with a ball if it landed in my hands, so I steer clear of things like softball and soccer. But cycling is a whole other story. I'm not sure whether it's the gliding motion or the wind splashing against my face, but cycling relaxes me. Cycling is what I do to get away from the world.

But as I turned into the cemetery, with the dew

still glistening on the grass and the sunlight barely peeking through the leafy trees, my shoulders were tensed up to my ears. I scuffed my Birkenstocks against the pavement to bring Mariposa to a stop while I unbuckled my helmet and looped it around my arm. As I began coasting down the steep incline that leads to Fall Creek, my hair whipped into my mouth and in front of my eyes, obstructing my vision. But I didn't care. Because for one split second, as I pedaled so fast I thought I'd lift off the earth, I'd been able to forget that this whole mess was happening.

✦　✦　✦

Kitty was already in front of Lincoln Street Diner by the time I arrived. She was leaning against the hood of her mom's station wagon, which is unofficially becoming her car. Clutching a handful of wilted dandelions, she was flicking their golden heads into the street with her thumb. Her long blond hair, still damp, hung loosely around her shoulders.

"Hey . . ." I stopped pedaling and let Mariposa roll the rest of the way to the curb.

"What happened to you?" Kitty asked as she tossed the flowers onto the sidewalk.

"What do you mean?"

"You look like you've come through a typhoon. Are you going for the wild child look?"

My hand wandered self-consciously to my hair, tucking wayward strands behind my ears.

"Here." Kitty reached into her pocket and produced a rubber band. "A ponytail cures all."

I hooked my helmet around my handlebars and gathered my hair back. As Kitty popped open the rear of the station wagon, I hoisted Mariposa into the folded-down seat.

"Much better." Kitty nodded approvingly. "Now you're presentable."

The diner was bustling with its morning crowd: a mix of townies, high-school kids and Cornell students. As the waitress gestured us to a booth near the back, some guys hunched over their coffee gaped at Kitty. She didn't seem to notice, or if she did, she's so accustomed to the attention that it didn't faze her.

Once the waitress had taken our order, Kitty rested her chin on her fists and sighed. "Is it just me or do the guys in our grade have yet to hit puberty?"

"What do you mean?" I asked, swirling the mound of whipped cream into my hot chocolate.

Kitty took a sip of coffee, which she started drinking this past winter. I personally find coffee repulsive, even when doctored up with milk and sugar. But Kitty explained that you have to grow accustomed to the taste, like with beer and chili peppers.

"When I was at that party last night, I noticed that half the sophomore boys don't even shave . . . or maybe just their mustaches." Kitty paused. "The seniors, on the other hand, they're already real men."

I almost said, *Easy for you to say when you've got one.* But instead I asked, "How was the party?"

"It was okay. Jack and I slipped out early and drove to his lake house, where we . . ."

Kitty paused, relishing the suspense. I lifted my hot chocolate to my lips.

". . . Did it in his parents' bed."

I coughed into my mug, spraying whipped cream onto the table. I quickly smudged it away with a napkin, which I then stuffed in my pocket. I don't know why Kitty and Jack's sexual escapades still throw me off balance. It's not like it's anything new; they've been official lovers for two months now.

Just a lot of pushing and sweating, Kitty had reported after they'd done it for the first time.

What was the best part? I'd whispered across our table in the snack bar, hardly able to grasp that my best friend was no longer a virgin.

At the end, when he let out this long groan, like a bull-

frog, Kitty had said. *It was all I could do not to burst out laughing.*

I'd nodded. It hadn't been quite the response I was looking for.

But now Kitty was sipping her coffee and describing how Jack wanted to "spice up our sex life."

I thought about cracking some joke, like *Jack must have renewed his subscription to* Glamour, but I knew Kitty wouldn't find it very funny. Either that or she'd call me *juvenile,* an adjective that she utters in the tone one generally reserves for pedophiles or granny's-purse-snatchers.

"Like how?" I asked, feeling a bit like a TelePrompTer.

Kitty leaned forward and in an exaggerated whisper mouthed, "He wants me to give him a you-know-what!"

I scrunched my eyebrows quizzically.

"I say, *dis*-gusting," Kitty continued, her lips curling back from her perfectly ivory, perfectly spaced, never-set-foot-in-an-orthodontist's-office teeth.

"Kitty?" I paused for a second. We the chaste, as much as we'd rather not admit it, often need things spelled out for us. "What's a 'you-know-what'?"

Kitty's back was to the grill, so she didn't see the waitress approaching, a tray balanced on her shoulder.

Just as Kitty prodded a finger toward her cheek, pushing her tongue against the inside of the other cheek in a rhythmic motion, the waitress plopped a plate of hash browns in front of her. Kitty's earlobes turned crimson, her pointer frozen in the universal "blow job" gesture. The waitress chuckled knowingly as she handed me my pancakes. I attempted to swallow the laughter mounting in my throat.

"Toothache?" the waitress asked her, grinning as she tossed the syrup onto the table.

And that's when I began to giggle maniacally, the way you do when someone's tickling you and you want to get them to stop but you still keep laughing. I turned to face the wall, hoping it would sober me up, but all it did was make me sputter harder.

Kitty looked mortified as she tip-tapped her manicured fingernails against the tabletop. "Really, Sammie," she hissed, "you're making a scene!"

I began to hiccup.

"Can I get you some water?" The waitress had started to walk away, but she stopped a few strides from our booth.

I nodded desperately, attempting to hold my breath.

A minute later, I plugged my nose as I slowly sipped the icy water.

"Well." Kitty sprinkled pepper over her potatoes in quick, jerking motions. "Let's hope that's all for today."

I attempted to respond, but when I opened my mouth all that came out was a loud hiccup.

✦ ✦ ✦

It was only on the drive back to my house that I realized Kitty hadn't asked me anything about the move. It had been all Kitty, Kitty, Kitty and Jack, Jack, Jack. Which would have been okay on any other day, but on the morning I'm abandoning my entire life, I think I deserve an extra helping of airtime.

Sometimes my relationship with Kitty confuses me. I feel like I slip into this "good friend" role with her. I'm always offering an ear, as if her life stories—without a doubt more action-packed—have more value than mine. And sometimes when I'm talking, I catch her eyes glazing over, so I wind up babbling quickly before I lose her attention.

As we pulled into the driveway, Kitty shifted the station wagon into park.

"I can't believe you're leaving," she said softly. "I'm going to miss you so much."

I unbuckled my seat belt and hopped out as Kitty

opened the back. Once I'd leaned Mariposa against a tree, Kitty and I gave each other a hug.

"Promise you'll call as soon as you get your number."

I nodded.

"And promise we'll visit this summer."

I nodded again.

"Oh, Sammie . . . I don't know what I'm going to do without you here." Kitty's voice cracked. "You've really sustained me over the years."

And then Kitty began to cry, not out loud, just little tears slipping down her pale cheeks. I fished the napkin out of my pocket and wiped them dry.

After I'd returned Mariposa to the garage, I opened the side door. Moxie bounded out to greet me, howling and prancing in circles.

"What's wrong, girl?" I asked, scratching behind her ears.

But as I entered the kitchen, I discovered what the commotion was about. Mom was slumped on a stool, her face buried in her hands. Shards of broken pottery were strewn across the tiled floor. I kicked myself for not using the front entrance and heading directly up to my room.

Mom wiped her nose with the back of her hand. "Dad and I bought this the summer we moved to Ithaca," she moaned.

Glancing at the debris, I recognized the remains of the midnight-blue bowl that we always filled with peaches in the summer and apples in the fall.

"I was wrapping it up when I heard Moxie barking in the yard . . . and I remembered I'd left her off her leash. . . ."

As Mom choked up again, I bounded up the stairs, two at a time. Once in my room, I dug my dictionary out of a city-bound crate and sat on my bed, thumbing through the S's.

Sustain: to support, hold . . . bear the weight of.

I sighed and flopped onto my back. As the dictionary slid off my legs in a waterfall of pages, I wondered if that was my eternal fate: to "support, hold and bear the weight of." And when it comes down to it, is there anyone out there who would do that for me?

CHAPTER FOUR

By the time the sun was directly overhead, I'd lugged my suitcases into the trunk of the Volvo and my crates onto the front porch for the movers to pick up. And I was halfway up the stairs with a broom when I remembered that the cleaning service was coming this afternoon. So when the Mayflower truck turned into the driveway, I was playing my guitar under the red maple in the backyard, doing my best imitation of a relaxed person.

But a few minutes later, the side door slammed and this guy stomped toward me. He was short, with wide shoulders and huge biceps. He reminded me of an inflatable punching bag.

"You live here?"

"Yeah . . ."

"We're going to need your help inside. That lady is driving my buddy crazy, handing him half-packed boxes and then taking them back to rewrap vases. At this rate, there's no way we're going to be on the road by one."

As he started back across the lawn, I stood up, brushing the grass off the back of my thighs. I could feel my cheeks tensing as I thought: *The Unmade Bed strikes again.*

An unmade bed. That's what Grandma Davis once called Mom. Not to her face, but while we were waiting in the driveway of my grandparents' San Jose ranch house, where Dad grew up. We'd risen early, to beat rush hour traffic to San Francisco, where we were meeting Aunt Jayne at Fisherman's Wharf. But we ended up leaving forty-five minutes late because Mom took forever to get ready, misplacing her sunglasses twice in the process.

Go easy on her, Beryl, Dad had said, calling Grandma Davis by her first name. As he shot a glance in my direction, I'd leaned down and double-knotted my sneakers, even though the laces rarely came undone.

Grandma Davis has never been crazy about Mom, and she doesn't work very hard to disguise it. Maybe it's because Grandma Davis is so rigid that you can set a clock by her. Maybe it has something to do with that theory about mothers never thinking any woman is good enough for their perfect sons. Or maybe it's because she wasn't invited to my parents' wedding, even though the only attendants were the justice of peace and a couple of witnesses, friends of Mom's from art school.

Before Mom was an art teacher, she used to dream of becoming a famous painter. But shortly after she'd moved into Dad's apartment near Columbia University, they'd discovered he was allergic to the fumes from her oil paints, so she'd tucked them away until they could afford studio space. When I was two, we headed up to Cornell, where Dad had been offered a teaching position. And somehow Mom's art took a backseat.

Not completely, like she had an easel set up in the garage, where Dad paid an electrician to install track lighting in one corner. Sometimes Mom would get so immersed in a canvas that she wouldn't emerge all weekend, except to sprint into the bathroom or grab a slice of the pizza Dad and I had ordered. When I was younger, I used to carry my paper plate out there and sit cross-legged on the cement floor, quietly watching her. I would feel this swelling inside as she leaped around, splashing colorful strokes, almost like a dancer. Several times, Mom would abandon the canvas before it was finished, descending into a funk until it mysteriously disappeared from the garage. *What's the use?* she'd responded gloomily when I inquired about the whereabouts of one I particularly liked: orange figures dancing in concentric circles around a purple sun. *Where's it going to get me, anyway?*

I think Mom blames Dad for taking her away from the urban scene and plunking her in Small Town, USA. Not that Ithaca isn't artsy; compared to neighboring communities, it's the cultural capital of the world. But it's not exactly where you come to make a name for yourself or connect with other painters. That was a recurring theme in Mom and Dad's arguments. Usually to the tune of Mom itching to leave Ithaca as soon as I go away to college. And Dad suggesting they start traveling more instead, that with the way things are going in academia, he couldn't risk walking out on Cornell.

I'll be the first to admit that Mom and Dad weren't hunky-dory, not for the past year or so. I guess I'd been hoping the sabbatical in California would jump-start things, with Dad researching a book on John Steinbeck and Mom looking into studios that provided live models. Hell, I'd even convinced myself that I could benefit from a change of scenery.

But this wasn't how it was supposed to happen, with Mom and the movers bickering about breakables, and

Moxie bounding around the house until I tied her in the backyard with a bowl of fresh water. Even though I'd applied two layers of deodorant, my underarms were already sweaty.

In the midst of everything the doorbell rang. It was the realtor, coming to pick up our house keys. Well, guess who arranged to drop them off at her agency on our way out of town. And guess who thought to call the cleaning service, requesting they come tomorrow morning rather than this afternoon. Definitely not the Unmade Bed!

✦ ✦ ✦

"At least we're heading east." Mom set her sunglasses on the dashboard. The sun was beginning its descent into the hills of southern New York.

I readjusted the radio. We'd only been on the road a hundred miles and this was the third time I'd had to locate a decent station.

"Because I'd hate to drive into the afternoon sun . . ."

Mom had been making intermittent comments for the whole trip, even though I was barely responding. I just didn't feel like gabbing as if it were any other day. Especially when we were pulling out of Ithaca. As I'd watched the familiar sights fade away, I'd wondered if Dad had felt a similar emptiness the morning Mom drove him to the airport. But then I'd pushed that thought out of my mind. After all, he'd made that bed for himself and now he was soundly sleeping in it.

"Do you think Moxie is okay?" Mom asked after several minutes. "Maybe we should stop at the next rest area."

I glanced back at Moxie, whose head was resting on her front paws. Her real name is Amoxicillin because Dad brought her to me when I was nine and had strep throat. But after explaining to the thousandth person why she was named after an antibiotic, we shortened it to Moxie, which is easier to holler across a park anyway.

A few miles later, Mom gestured to a gas station off to the right. "I'm going to stop here."

I didn't respond as she pulled up to the pump and shut off the engine.

"Look." Mom glanced sideways at me. "I'm going through a lot too."

As I unbuckled my seat belt, Mom clamped her hand over mine.

"All I ask is that you act civil."

I hopped out of the car. As Moxie bounded toward the Dumpsters, I slammed my door a lot harder than necessary.

Act civil, act civil. I stewed, pacing around the pavement. When haven't I acted civil? Would someone please tell me the crime in wanting silence for a few hours? Out of the corner of my eye, I noticed two college students hopping into a pickup truck parked at the other pump. Wouldn't Mom flip out if she returned to the car and I'd hitched a ride with them? Off into the sunset. Anywhere but New York City.

Mom didn't say anything as she turned back onto Route 17. She just balanced a cup of coffee between her legs and tossed me a bag of Ritz Bits and an iced tea. Even though I hadn't eaten for hours, I didn't feel hungry. I didn't feel thirsty. All I felt was drained. I rested my head against the seat.

The next thing I knew it was dark and all I could see were oncoming headlights. I glanced around, feeling pangs in my stomach. I had no idea where we were. I opened the crackers and popped a few in my mouth.

As we approached a sign for the George Washington Bridge, Mom sucked in her breath.

"What?" I asked, freezing midchew.

"Don't you see?" Mom gestured toward the Manhattan skyline in the distance.

As I surveyed the crescendo of glittering lights, I felt an impending sense of doom. Somewhere in that enormous spectacle of architecture, Mom and I are going to live.

"We've made it, Sammie." Mom was wiping her teary eyes with a crooked finger. "We've come home."

If it hadn't been for the iced tea, I might have choked to death on the crackers in my throat. Which wouldn't have been an altogether bad thing, because then I never would have had to set foot in Apartment 806.

✦ ✦ ✦

Apartment 806 was smaller than Mom had described and reeked of fresh paint. It essentially consisted of two adjacent boxes, each of which could have fit into our family room in Ithaca. A narrow entranceway led into Box #1, which contained the tiny excuse for a kitchen, a wooden table with two chairs and the old futon from our guest room. My new sleeping quarters. And Box #2, where the movers had deposited Mom's bed and desk, led to the pink-tiled bathroom. So in order to go pee or get a glass of juice from the fridge, one of us would have to trek right through the other's "bed-room."

As Mom began opening windows, Moxie nervously sniffed every inch of the apartment. The movers had scattered our belongings around the rooms, and in two sweaty trips, Mom and I had hauled our suitcases up from the car, dumping them in the entranceway. It was truly a disaster area. A claustrophobic little disaster area.

Welcome home, I said under my breath. *Welcome to the dollhouse.*

Pushing some plastic hangers off the corner of the futon, I let my knees fall out from under me. My hands felt clammy. My head felt woozy. I rested it between my knees and attempted some deep, steady breaths.

"It may look like a mess now," Mom grunted as she yanked open a window, "but it has a lot of possibilities."

"Possibilities?"

"Well, for one thing, look at the view."

"The view?"

"It doesn't help if you repeat everything I say."

"I'm not repeating every . . . ," I started, but caught myself.

Mom began peeling back the tape on a box labeled *linens.*

"It's been a long day . . . why don't we just make our beds and get some sleep?"

I sat there for a second watching her.

"At least you can help me," she snapped.

There she goes. I sighed. *Mom Jekyll and Mom Hyde.*

As I leaped over some loose boards on the floor, I

tripped, stubbing my toe. The horrible kind of stub where the nail separates from the skin.

"Owww," I yelped, hopping around on one foot.

Mom had been so preoccupied she hadn't even noticed.

"Owowow," I said louder, my toe pulsing in agony.

"I don't understand why you're not—"

And that's when I interrupted her. Enough was enough! The rim of my toenail was filling with blood.

"Because I hate it here!" I shouted.

Mom froze in midair, blue-flowered sheets in hand. As she flung them onto the futon, a thundercloud settled over her face. "There's a pillow in that crate . . . do your own damn bed for all I care."

Then she stormed into the other room and hurled the door shut. Sinking back onto the futon, I felt dizzy from the pain. Either that or the paint fumes.

Great. Not in the apartment fifteen minutes and already a catastrophe. Really great.

After several minutes, I limped over to my suitcase and dug out my nightgown and my toiletries bag, brushing my teeth at the kitchen sink. I didn't have the energy to pull down the futon, so I spread the bottom sheet across the surface and bunched up my T-shirt for a pillow. Collapsing onto the lumpy mattress, I pulled the other sheet on top of me.

I lay there for a long time, listening to the honking and car alarms on the street below. I could hear someone puttering in the hallway outside our apartment. I hopped out of bed to double-check that Mom had locked the door. Dodging boxes on my way back to the futon, I paused in front of the window and stared out at the panorama of lighted apartments. I could actually see right into plenty of them. Real things, like StairMasters and televisions flickering, and the occasional figure walking from room to room. I began to wonder whether, if I looked long enough, I could actually catch people undressing, or even having sex.

Speaking of sex, breakfast with Kitty already feels like a year ago. All that talk about spicing up her lovemaking, like she was Aphrodite incarnate. I have to admit it made me jealous, though I'd never give her the satisfaction of knowing that.

I wonder if a guy will ever want to sleep with me, or if I have a neon sign on my forehead that says "untouchable," only it doesn't show up in the mirror and no one wants to hurt my feelings by telling me. Sometimes, when I'm reading an erotic scene in a novel, I can imagine what it will feel like to have sex. And it's not like in the movies, perfectly scripted, in front of a blazing fire. It's different, more sensual somehow. I hope my first time is with someone I love. I hope it's his first time too. I hope we're not collecting our Social Security checks yet. I hope we can laugh out loud if either of us groans like a bullfrog.

As I slid back under the sheet, I ran my hands along the curves of my breasts and stomach. Sometimes it still surprises me that I no longer have a girl's body. That at some point over the past few years, woman-hood has crept up on me, complete with hips, hairs and Grand Tetons. It reminds me of hide-and-seek, when It calls out, *Ready or not, here I come,* even if you haven't found a safe place to duck away yet. Ready or not, the game has begun. And there's nothing you can do to stop it.

CHAPTER FIVE

If our first night in New York City was bad, the ensuing days made it look like a whirlwind trip to Disney World. In fact, I've composed this mental letter to *The Guinness Book of World Records:*

Dear Record Keeper:

I'm writing to request consideration for "Three Most Horrible Consecutive Days." If you don't already have this category, I recommend you create it immediately and make me your charter member. Here's why:

1. *Our first morning in Manhattan, I went downstairs to walk the dog, only to discover a traffic cop slipping a ticket under the windshield wiper of our car. I tried to*

explain how we just moved here, but she pointed to an "alternate side parking" sign two feet away and launched into a ten-minute lecture about complying with street cleaning rules. And I don't even have my license yet! What's more, when I handed the ticket to my mom, she got upset that I didn't explain how we just moved here.

2. Speaking of dogs, there's this law that you have to scoop up after them, even in Central Park, which is right near our apartment. I found this out upon exiting the scene of the crime, when a complete stranger launched into a ten-minute lecture about complying with doggy-doo rules. I'm beginning to think I'm in a police state! Of course, I had no Baggies on hand, so I had to rummage through a nearby trash bin for a newspaper. If I had stock in a soap company, I'd be a millionaire by now.

3. Speaking of complying with rules, our eighth-floor apartment adheres to the "heat rises" law of nature. It's stuffy and sweltering and other than this tiny metal fan, the only draft we get is when someone exhales. The building superintendent, who everyone refers to as "the super," offered to install an air conditioner for a nominal fee, to which my mom replied, "No thanks . . . synthetic air gives me a headache." **Synthetic air?**

4. Speaking of my mom, she has metamorphosed into a toy mouse that's been wound too tight. She's attempting to make up for her fourteen-year hiatus from the city by

*doing and seeing and tasting everything she reads about
in the newspaper. At once. With me. So even though
we've barely unpacked our suitcases, we've already gone
to two gallery openings, a tenement museum, a
restaurant where everything contains peanut butter, a
Brazilian street fair and a free opera in the park, to
name a few. And we've probably trekked enough to have
circumnavigated a small country by now. Ditto for stock
in Band-Aids, if you get my drift.*

*I could go on forever, but I'm sure you have your hands full
assessing the largest potato in Idaho. I'd offer my phone
number, in case you needed to check facts, but my mom
forgot to ask Bell Atlantic to hook up a jack beforehand.
Now they're saying it won't happen until the early part of
next week, if we're lucky. Do we sound lucky to you?*

*In desperation,
Samantha L. Davis*

✦　✦　✦

In order to plead a strong case, I wouldn't include this
in my letter, but there is one redeeming factor about
New York City: I like our building. It's the tallest on the
block and red brick, with marigolds around the trees in
front. The super sprays them with a hose every evening
so the water can soak in overnight rather than be dried
up by the heat of the day.

The super lives on the first floor with his wife, whom everyone calls Mama. They're in their sixties and from the Dominican Republic, which is the eastern half of an island in the Caribbean. Mama doesn't even speak English. I mentioned to the super that I've taken Spanish for two years, so whenever I see him in the lobby, he asks, *¿Como estás?* to which I respond, *Muy bien.* It's nothing more than *How are you?* and *Fine,* but it's still pretty cool. I bet Ms. Guerrero would be proud, especially since she used to emphasize that the only way to learn a foreign language is to be immersed in the culture. Which always seemed like an odd thing for a Spanish teacher to tell a class full of kids in Ithaca.

The super was the one who told me how to get to the roof, by riding the elevator to the top floor and taking the stairs the rest of the way. As I ventured up on the fourth day, I didn't realize what a treat I was in for. I mean, it's just an ordinary rooftop, covered with metal panels and strips of tar. And I'm lucky I'm not scared of heights, because there's only a short brick wall running around the perimeter. But the view was spectacular. Buildings as far as the eye could see, the Hudson River to the west and beyond that, New Jersey.

Later that evening, I grabbed my guitar and headed up again to catch the tail end of the sunset. The metal rooftop was still warm from the sun. As I sat there finger-picking an Alanis song I'd just heard on the radio, I felt a sense of peacefulness. This was probably the first moment I'd slowed down since we arrived in New York City, what with Mom's frenetic pace. It's not like I'm this slovenly spoilsport; I just needed time to digest all the changes. Mom has opted for the plunge-head-first-into-pool method, with me strapped to her back. I'm beginning to think I'm a victim of her most recent acquisition, *Reinventing Your Life*. When she toted it home from the bookstore on our first day, I just shook my head. I'm sure self-help works wonders for some people, as long as they understand that miracles don't happen overnight.

I strummed a G-A-D chord progression. The sky was growing so dark I could barely see my fingers. I began to feel an aching in my gut, some blend of lonely and nervous and empty. It reminded me of when I was nine and spent a forlorn week at this YMCA camp on Keuka Lake. Only then it was classic homesickness. Much harder to diagnose this time around, seeing that my physical *home* is presently overrun with Oscar Mayer Wieners and half of my parental unit is seven floors below me.

Maybe it's Ithaca that I miss. I wonder what Kitty is doing right now. Probably hanging out with Jack, seeing a movie at the mall. And what about Dad, three thousand miles away? Does he even know we've arrived in Manhattan? I wonder if Mom has called from a pay phone to tell him. I sure haven't, even though he mailed me his new number right after he arrived in California, along with an embroidered blouse for my birthday.

When I saw it in Berkeley, I thought of you immediately, Dad had written in the card, which I'd tucked in the back of my dictionary. I considered cutting the shirt into tiny pieces and ramming it down the garbage disposal, but instead I folded it into a corner of a duffel bag. So now, as with all my belongings, it's stirred into one of the many piles strewn across the apartment.

On Tuesday afternoon, I was just tackling a heap of winter clothes when Mom demanded that I accompany her to the grocery store for our first big shop. Thus far we've been subsisting on fruit, bagels and Chinese takeout, but we have yet to stock up on staples. *Staples.* Up until a few weeks ago, I'd never given a second thought to the sugar in the cupboard or the soap in the shower. I'd just assumed they'd be there.

Everything was okay at first. I pushed the metal cart through the brightly lit aisles, and Mom tossed in various items, commenting how the prices here were double those of Ithaca. But as we approached the Tex-Mex section, Mom's voice grew progressively louder.

"Can you keep it down a little?" I whispered. "It's no big deal."

"No big deal?" she boomed. "It's not like we have money galore."

First synthetic air and now money galore! Where was Mom coming up with these phrases? I glanced around. The only person in sight was a middle-aged woman reading the nutritional value on a bottle of salsa.

I felt my throat constricting. So money was now an issue? I mean, we were never rolling in it in Ithaca, but we could pretty much afford whatever we needed. And we always took a yearly vacation, even if it was just to California or West Palm Beach, where Mom's mother lives. Before the trial separation, I remember hearing talk about Mom not working during Dad's sabbatical year so she could concentrate on her art. I guess that plan has flown out the window along with all the others. Mom has already been poring through the help-wanteds for teaching gigs, and even went to a copy shop this morning to fax her résumé to a few places. It felt strange when she asked for my input on the cover letters, commenting about how painting was much more her forte than writing.

By the time Mom and I arrived at the counter, our cart was so full that the checkout lady suggested we pay extra for delivery. As she quoted the fee, Mom let out a low whistle. I eyed the three teenage girls in line behind us and prayed Mom wouldn't pull another doozie out of her choice-phrase satchel.

True to form, Mom pointed to me and bellowed, "I have my own personal delivery service."

I began thumbing through *People* as if I was about to take a pop quiz on celebrity weddings.

On the way home, both of us outfitted with more bags than a pack mule, I walked a few strides behind Mom. Not that I was even trying to; Mom has adopted this power walk since we arrived in Manhattan, a pace that is literally and figuratively hard to match. Especially with the blisters that have bubbled up on my feet, even though I've been wearing my beat-up old sneakers night and day.

Upon reaching our building, Mom shot in ahead of me. I caught the door an inch shy of closing. As I entered the lobby, she disappeared into the elevator.

"At least you could have held . . . ," I started to say, but as I approached the automated doors, I stopped short. Mom wasn't the only person inside. And not only that, but the other person happened to be the most gorgeous guy I've ever seen in my entire life.

"Got it?" he asked me, releasing the *door open* button and pushing 15, the top floor.

I tried to speak but no sound came out.

As the doors closed, I attempted to hide the fact that I was staring at him. He was in his midtwenties, with shoulder-length black hair and angular cheekbones dotted with enough stubble to put Kitty's senior men to shame. And his lips. I could have written a dissertation about those lips. Moist. Succulent. Very kisser-friendly.

He was also a dead ringer for Johnny Depp, who I happen to think is the sexiest person alive, even though Kitty pointed out that he's old enough to be my father.

It's not like I'm planning to marry him, I responded. *But even if I was, plenty of May-December relationships work out fine.*

Sure, if you've got a thing for drool, dentures and Depends, Kitty pshawed.

My legs were shaking so hard I was convinced Johnny Depp could tell. I glanced down. *Omigod.* Why had I never noticed before that my beat-up old sneakers made my feet look huge?

"You just move in?"

Hearing J.D.'s voice made me jump. I opened my mouth to respond. Again no sound.

"Yeah." Mom pressed the button for the eighth floor. "Thursday night."

J.D.'s chest muscles rippled through his thin T-shirt. I was tempted to reach over and stroke them. Instead I watched the floor numbers light up. Four . . . five . . . three more to go. *Omigod. J.D. just peeked at my breasts!* I tried to relax my mouth, but it's times like these when I develop amnesia, suddenly forgetting what to do with my face, my hands, everything. Why hadn't I worn my slinky black tank top that reveals every curve, rather than this baggy T-shirt that makes the rest of my girth appear as supple as my C-cups? Kitty's always saying that if you want people to buy your apples, you've got to put them out for sale.

Melons too? I once asked her.

Even watermelons, she said, smirking, as I whacked her arm.

"Are you two sisters?" J.D. was looking from Mom to me.

I glanced at Mom. Those deep circles under her eyes still haven't gone away, even though we've been in Manhattan for nearly a week. I gripped my bags tightly, wishing the elevator would hurry up and arrive at our floor.

"No." Mom laughed. "This is my daughter. She's just sixteen."

Omigod! Blood rushed to my cheeks. Where was the button that could evaporate me into thin air?

As the elevator opened, Mom turned and said, "By the way, I'm Roz and this is Sammie."

"Sammie." J.D. grinned. "Nice."

Nice what? Nice name? Nice boobs? Sneaking one last look as the doors were closing, I could have sworn he winked at me. *Omigodgodgod!*

"Nice guy," Mom murmured, unlocking the door. "He looks like that movie star. I can't place him, though."

I made sure to keep my mouth shut. Next thing I know she'd probably go and tell him that as well.

✦   ✦   ✦

Seconds after we entered the apartment, disaster struck. Moxie, who still isn't accustomed to being holed up in two rooms, stampeded out to greet us. As she lunged forward, I attempted to sidestep her, stumbled and spilled one of my bags. And guess what should fly out and hurtle to the floor, smashing into pieces—the liter of olive oil, of course.

"Shit!" Mom and I shouted at the same time.

Moxie careened under the futon, tail between her legs.

As a yellow pool of oil spread over the hardwood

floor, I dashed into the kitchen in search of paper towels. We hadn't gotten any yet, so I grabbed a dish towel and threw it over the spill, which nearly sent Mom into a tailspin.

"What was I supposed to use, toilet paper?" I snapped.

After twenty minutes of scrubbing and sopping and gingerly picking up splinters of glass, I decided to take a shower. I felt disgustingly greasy. I never wanted to see another bottle of olive oil as long as I lived.

I started up the water as soon as I was in the bathroom. Catching sight of myself in the mirror, I frowned. My hair looked so stringy. I hope it was from the oil. I hope it didn't look like that in the elevator. I hope J.D. didn't notice.

J.D. My stomach flipped over as I began to undress, stuffing my dirty clothes into the laundry bag.

Maybe we'll run into each other on the roof one day, start talking, really hit it off. And I don't just mean small talk . . . we'll go below the surface. He'll listen to what I have to say and then he'll tell me about his work, but not as if I'm a kid. It will be adult to adult.

You don't seem sixteen. He'll shake his head.

Age is just numbers, I'll say. *It's the person inside that counts.*

That's deep, Sammie, he'll say, gazing into my eyes.

J.D. won't notice the "untouchable" sign on my fore-head. No, he'll find me sexy. Sexy and irresistible. He'll be my first lover, gently nibbling my neck, whispering in my ear. Afterward, as I snuggle in his sinewy arms, he'll think how lucky he is to have met someone like me. How most women out there are so jaded.

The bathroom was getting steamy. Bare naked, I swiped my hand across the foggy mirror and studied my reflection.

"Hi, J.D.," I said huskily.

Pushing my breasts together, I tilted my head to one side and puffed up my lips, like those Victoria's Secret models always do.

"How do you like these, J.D.?"

Not so bad, I thought, pulling aside the curtain and stepping into the shower. *Not so bad after all.*

CHAPTER SIX

"Are you almost ready?" Mom hollered from the bath-room, where she was drenching herself with a vanilla spray that she'd picked up at some boutique yesterday.

I didn't answer. I was crouched next to the stereo, blasting "Both Sides Now." That's this amazing Joni Mitchell song—just voice and acoustic guitar—about coming to terms with growth and change. I've never listened to her music much before, but I stumbled across this CD during the move. It must have been Dad's. He's crazy about Joni, from back when he was in college. Supposedly, he wanted to name me Chelsea, after her song "Chelsea Morning."

I wouldn't mind being a Chelsea. *Chelsea Leigh Davis.*

Chelsea Leigh Davis would be equal parts poise and intrigue. Chelsea Leigh Davis would swivel her hips, toss her tendrils of hair and look a guy in the eye when talking to him. Chelsea Leigh Davis would flash her captivating smile upon entering a room, making people lust for her story, not to mention her body.

"I didn't hear you." Mom's voice was louder this time. "Are you almost ready?"

"Yessss!" I shouted back.

Joni was singing about looking at clouds from both sides now.

"I can leave anytime," I added.

We're going to the Rosenthals' for dinner. Shira Rosenthal was Mom's college roommate, back when she was Shira Krantz. But ten years ago, Shira's husband died suddenly of a brain aneurysm, leaving her with two small children: Eli, around my age, and Becca, then a baby.

Shira is a social worker at a home for delinquent teenagers. You'd think a profession like that would drain someone, but whenever she calls she's always upbeat, often talking so loudly I have to hold the phone away from my ear. I should know. We spoke several times this spring, when Mom was trying to place me in a good public school. Shira knew an administrator at Beacon—Eli's artsy high school—who pulled some strings to get me in at the last minute.

"Moons and Junes and Ferris wheels," sang Joni, "that dizzy dancing way you feel . . ."

I rewound the CD a few bars. *What amazing imagery!* I understand exactly what Joni is referring to, like she's talking directly to me. I'd love to know "Both Sides Now" by heart. It sounds like it would be a cinch to learn on guitar, but it's actually rhythmically complicated, the sort of song where I used to ask for Dad's help. He would set down his book, grumbling something about how Bob Dylan didn't tear *his* father from Melville. But after a few minutes, Dad would be so engrossed I'd have to pry my guitar from his grasp, teasing him that *Dylan* became the folk music legend, not Herman Melville.

Mom appeared in the doorway, wearing only a magenta bra and bikini underwear set, a towel turban-wrapped about her hair. Her stomach swells out a little and her hips are the birthing variety, like mine, but for someone who's going to turn forty-three in a few weeks, Mom's got a fairly decent body. Sometimes it seems like she gets more visual ravishings from guys in the street than I do. Which is depressing, seeing that I'm supposed to be at the prime of something in my life, I just haven't figured out what yet. As Mom began rummaging through our shared closet, I looked away. We didn't used to strip in front of each other.

"It's a fifteen-minute walk up there," Mom said, "and I told Shira we'd arrive at six-thirty."

I glanced at the clock on the VCR: *6:10 P.M.* No problemo. We'll leave in five minutes.

Mom pulled a black linen sundress over her head. I slipped my feet into my Birkenstocks, careful not to disturb the blister lurking on my pinkie toe.

Joni was recalling how she really didn't know life at all, when Mom turned and gave me an elongated once-over, like I was a side of beef she was considering buying at a farm auction. If she weren't a vegetarian, of course.

"Is that what you're going to wear?" she asked, scrunching her nose disapprovingly.

"Yeah." I glanced down at my khaki shorts and pale blue T-shirt. "Do you have a problem with it?"

"It looks like you just dug that shirt from the bottom of a pile."

I swiped my hand across my chest, smoothing out the cotton. "And you think Becca and Eli will notice a few wrinkles?" I asked. My stomach flip-flopped when I said their names.

"I don't like that tone of voice, Sammie." Mom was

jerking a comb through her wet hair, spraying pellets of water against the full-length mirror. "You haven't seen them in years. I told you how much they've grown up . . . maybe you can give them the illusion that you have too."

As soon as Mom said that, I instantly regressed to twelve. I scowled. I stalked over to the closet. I flung aside hangers as loudly as possible.

Mom had crashed at Shira's while she was apartment-hunting, but I haven't seen the Rosenthals since this long weekend four summers ago when our families rented a cottage together in the Adirondacks. It had rained for three straight days so we'd holed up indoors, playing a marathon Monopoly game. Until Becca landed on Eli's Boardwalk and, in a flurry of tears, cards and little plastic houses, flung the board into the air. As Shira steered her into the stairwell for a talking-to, I was stranded alone with Eli, who still hadn't enhanced his two-word vocabulary of *hey* (meaning everything from *hello* to *I-want-more-cookie-dough-ice-cream*) and *naw* (meaning *not-on-your-life, leave-me-alone*).

That is, until the last morning, when the sun finally broke through the clouds and we rented a motorboat to go waterskiing on a nearby lake. After failing miserably at getting up, I swam over to the boat and unbuckled my life vest. To my horror, my bathing suit top had come undone. I dove underwater to fasten it again but it was too late. When I came up, Eli, sputtering like a locomotive, crooned *LifeSavers, LifeSavers, LifeSavers.* Of course, no one else caught on, and Mom even had the audacity to offer him some TicTacs from her bag, which plunged him into further gales of laughter.

I finally decided on my slinky black tank top. It's a slippery material, some kind of cotton-spandex blend, so it can pass for dressy or casual. And it never, ever wrinkles. I stomped over to the mirror, where Mom was working a palmful of gel into her hair. As I approached, I noticed that she reeked of vanilla musk.

"Satisfied?" I asked, draping the tank top in front of my T-shirt.

Mom quickly darted her head sideways. "Can't you do better than that? Maybe a nice skirt . . . a little jewelry at your neck—"

"At least I don't smell like cake batter," I said. I couldn't help it. It just slipped out.

"What's that supposed to mean?"

I took a step backward.

"Are you saying I've sprayed on too much?" Mom sniffed down the front of her dress.

"All I was saying"—I spoke slowly, careful to select the right words—"is that you smell very vanilla."

"It *is* too strong." Mom yanked her dress over her

head, flung it on the bed and dashed into the bath-room, mumbling something about never making it by six-thirty now.

As I heard the shower start up again, I tugged on the tank top, which felt tighter than usual around my chest. I studied my reflection in the mirror and attempted a deep breath, but my throat felt tight. Chelsea Leigh Davis wouldn't be nervous about going to the Rosenthals' tonight. Chelsea Leigh Davis wouldn't worry about Eli dredging up the LifeSavers incident. But then again, Chelsea Leigh Davis's LifeSavers wouldn't have morphed into Grand Tetons, on display for the whole world to see.

CHAPTER SEVEN

"Sammie! You look so grown up! Roz! What a great dress!" Shira was waiting outside the elevator when the doors opened to their floor. She looked exactly the same as four years ago. Medium-length curly hair that bounced when she spoke, tortoiseshell glasses, sturdy frame draped with loose cotton clothing.

As she ushered us into the apartment, she slid her arms around Mom and me and breathed in deeply.

"Mmmm . . . vanilla!"

"Oh, God." Mom's voice tensed. "Is it obvious?"

Shira smiled. "Not at all. It's perfect."

I sniffed, but all I could smell was lasagna and something else, maybe garlic bread. Mom apologized for arriving late, but Shira dismissed it with a snap of her wrist.

"Eli and Becca have been *soooo* excited to see you!" Shira exclaimed as she steered us down the hallway.

I glanced into the living room, where Eli and Becca were slumped on the sofa watching MTV, looking anything but *soooo* excited to see us. Eli flicked off the power with the remote control.

"Becca *Rose*," Becca sang as she flipped her kinky red hair off her shoulders. The last time I'd seen her it had been chopped short, making her look like Orphan Annie.

Shira rolled her eyes. "All week it's Becca Rose *this* and Becca Rose *that*. . . ."

"That's going to be my stage name"—Becca grinned, exposing a mouthful of braces—"when I'm a famous gymnast!"

"Becca, Eli." Mom tucked her hair behind her ear and for a second I saw her mouth twitch nervously. "You remember Samantha?"

Samantha?!? Is this my punishment for refusing to change into a *nice skirt*? I'd conceded with the jewelry, borrowing Mom's black coral necklace, but had put my foot down when it came to an article of clothing that evoked daisies, pleats and my first-grade class picture.

Becca made a face. *"Samantha?"*

I thought about saying *That's her obedient daughter, the one who wears nice skirts,* but instead I half-waved and stared down at my Birkenstocks. A flap of skin had rubbed off my colossal blister on the way here, leaving me to limp the final half dozen blocks.

"Isn't it Sammie?" Becca pressed.

I nodded.

"To quote Eli"—Becca leaped onto the cushions and waggled her small fist in the air— " 'You must fight the establishment!' I refuse to call you anything but Sammie!"

"Off the couch." Shira failed to disguise her smile. "Your feet are filthy."

"Isn't that right?" Becca settled back down again, needling Eli's arm.

Eli grunted as he fiddled with the remote control.

I glanced at Eli out of the corner of my eye. He was what Kitty would have deemed *crunchy granola*. His dark hair was bobbed, in a tangly sort of way, and he was wearing a raggedy T-shirt with green lettering that said REDUCE REUSE RECYCLE in a triangle with arrows connecting them. Ithaca was full of granolas: girls who didn't shave their legs; guys who espoused veganism. When I told Kitty that I thought one of them was cute—a banjo-playing loner with a mop of blond white-boy dreads—she teased me that she was going to have to start patrolling my locker for brewer's yeast.

"What can I get you to drink?" Shira asked. "Juice? Soda?"

I shifted my weight off the blistered foot. "Soda's fine with me."

"We have ginger ale, Coke, Diet Sprite . . ."

"I'll just have ginger ale."

"Me too," said Eli.

"Me three," Becca chimed in.

"Since when are you two guests around here?" Shira shrugged. "Roz?"

"I'll come in and help."

As they disappeared down the hall, I sat on the edge of a plush chair, slipping my feet in and out of my sandals. I swear, I must have been absent the day they taught small talk. Kitty would know exactly what to say at a time like this. She'd have everyone wrapped around her finger, begging for more.

I picked up the Impressionist art book from the side table and began perusing the pages.

After a minute, Becca asked if I liked being here so far.

I glanced up. I wasn't sure if she meant New York City or their apartment. "I guess," I said, taking refuge in the vague.

Eli grabbed a handful of crackers from the platter on the coffee table. I could hear him crunching away.

Becca flung a cheddar-cheese goldfish in the air and caught it in her mouth. Mom and Shira arrived with a tray of drinks. Mom handed us our ginger ales, and Shira wedged herself between Becca and Eli on the sofa. As Mom settled into the other chair, across the room from me, I noticed her eyes were reddish and watery.

"Dig in!" Shira gestured to the coffee table.

I leaned over and cut myself a slice of Brie, balancing it on a whole-wheat cracker.

Mom began describing her job search. How since we didn't have a phone yet she'd had to include in her cover letters something to the effect of don't-call-me-I'll-call-you.

Shira laughed as she sipped at her glass of wine. "Any interviews set up yet?"

Mom held up three fingers. "They're all later this week."

I was just reaching for another cracker when I noticed Eli watching me. He quickly looked away.

A few minutes later, as Mom and Shira were discussing employment prospects, I peeked at Eli. His face looked about the same as last time, maybe a little older, and he actually had really nice eyes. Blue with long, dark lashes. But then he glanced over, catching me in the act. I feigned fascination with the cover of the art book.

"Sammie." Shira slipped off her glasses, allowing them to dangle from a beaded chain around her neck. "I can't believe how much you've grown. The last time I saw you, you were . . ."

My face heated up as her voice trailed off. I know she's talking about my chest. *Grown* is such an adult way of saying *you've been through puberty*.

If I had any prayer of Eli forgetting about LifeSavers, I'm sure it's front and center now. Why hadn't I stayed in my T-shirt rather than this slinky black tank top that reveals every curve? I set my ginger ale on its coaster and crossed my arms in front of me.

"When was that, Roz?" Shira was shaking her head. "Was that the trip to Raquette Lake?"

A buzzer went off in the kitchen.

"Lasagna's done." Shira hopped up, securing her glasses back on her face. "Let's eat while it's hot!"

Saved by the bell.

Becca flew off the sofa and bolted after her. Mom followed, asking if there was anything she could do to help.

My arms were still locked in front of me when Eli stood up. That's when I noticed how much taller he'd gotten, at least five or six inches, but he looked like he hadn't gained a pound. He wasn't emaciated exactly, but he was pretty skinny.

"You'll meet a lot of nice people at Beacon." Eli slurred all his words together, so it took me a second to realize that he was talking about his school. *Ah-hem.* Our school.

"Thanks," I said, picking some crumbs off my napkin and putting them in my mouth.

Eli smiled shyly as he scooped up a few more crackers. I noticed he had a dimple in his right cheek.

We were almost done with dinner when Mom started asking Eli about his interest in saving the planet.

"Eli's a tree hugger," Becca cried out, wrapping her arms around her body. There was a piece of lettuce stuck in her braces, but no one else seemed to notice.

"Becca." Shira shot her a stern look as she handed me the garlic bread.

"Becca *Rose.*"

Shira ignored Becca this time. "Tell them about it, Eli."

Eli wrung his cloth napkin in his hands as he muttered, "What's there to tell?"

"You just went to the Clearwater Revival," Shira prompted.

"Only for a weekend."

"And you're volunteering at the Central Park gardens this summer."

"Only a few afternoons a week."

I broke off a piece of bread and passed the basket to Mom. I felt sorry for Eli. I'd hate to be on the spot like that.

"And you're camping at Bear Mountain with Max and Ellen for a weekend in August," Shira said, more to Mom than to Eli.

Eli stared down at his lap.

"He did it last summer too. Max is my brother Jerry's son. You remember Jerry, Roz?"

Mom nodded.

"Max and his girlfriend took Eli and a couple friends up there last summer, to hike on some trails. They had a blast!"

I took a bite of my salad and listened quietly.

Just then, Mom blurted out, "That sounds like the kind of thing Sammie would like to do."

I froze midchew.

"Oh, Sammie," Shira gasped, "you should go with them! You'd love it! Max and Ellen are wonderful! They'll both be seniors at Rutgers and they've been together for over two years!"

Mom was nodding enthusiastically. My cheeks were heating up again as I attempted to gauge Eli's reaction, but he was consuming his lasagna as if he were going into hibernation for the winter. Who do they think I am? A charity case? A loser who can't make friends for herself? I'll show them who needs handouts! Just like that old Simon and Garfunkel song: *I have no need for friendship . . . friendship causes pain. . . .*

The phone started ringing.

Shira sprang up and bounded toward the kitchen.

Saved by the bell, part two.

I finally swallowed my salad.

When Shira returned, she was toting a tray with five bowls of chocolate mousse. My stomach felt so bloated I slipped my hands under the table and unsnapped my shorts.

"Who called?" Becca asked a few minutes later. Her braces were coated in chocolate.

"It was Grandpa. I said we'd call back at nine so you could wish him happy Father's Day." Shira pushed a napkin at Becca. "And swallow before you talk next time."

My heart dropped to my stomach. *Today was Father's Day?* That had completely passed me by, partially because our calendar was still in some crate. But also, what did I have to thank my father for this year? Messing up my life and betraying my trust? I'm sure they have tons of cards for *that* one.

Shira must have read something on my face because she reached across the table and patted my arm. "We don't pay much attention to Father's Day around here," she said.

"It's all about making money anyway," Eli said quickly, without looking up, "so damn Hallmarky."

I felt the chocolate mousse working its way up my throat.

Mom's spoon clanked loudly as she dropped it into her porcelain bowl.

Becca giggled and sang, "When you care enough to send the very best!"

✦ ✦ ✦

Mom and I didn't say a word to each other as we walked home along Central Park West. I kept thinking about Father's Day last year. Kitty had slept over the night before because she was joining us on a day hike at Watkins Glen. On the drive home, we had devoured an entire bag of Doritos as we sang along with the soundtrack from *Grease*. I'd teased Dad because he couldn't stay on key.

Jimmy D., I'd drawled, imitating my Texan chorus instructor, *may I suggest you just mouth the words?*

Dad had belly-laughed, which made the car veer over the white line.

Watch out, Jimmy D.! Kitty and I had shrieked from the backseat, clutching each other's hands.

Dad's name is James Davis, so I used to call him

Jimmy D. as a joke. Especially since Dad, while not the antithesis of James Dean, is definitely pretty academic. Rebel without an *Oxford English Dictionary*.

Just as we entered the lobby, Mom finally spoke.

"I can give you my credit card number if you want to call him from a pay phone," she said.

So she'd been thinking about it too. I shook my head. "No thanks."

The elevator arrived in the lobby. There was an older man inside, coming up from the basement with his laundry bag. After he stepped off at the third floor, Mom began massaging her temples.

"I really miss Dad," she said softly.

I didn't respond. Mom and I hadn't discussed Dad much since we'd been in New York City. When we did, it was ancient history stuff, like: *Remember that time Dad's students showed up to rake our leaves when he broke his ankle?* But neither of us seemed willing to broach the trial separation, almost like if we didn't talk about it, it hadn't happened. So when Mom said she missed him, it caught me off guard. As I studied her face, it struck me how painful this was for her too. How, in some ways, Mom and I are marooned on the same deserted island. Together, yet so alone.

I reached over and lightly touched her arm.

"I feel a headache coming on." Mom was squinting. She didn't seem to notice my fingers on her forearm. "I'm going to take some aspirin and get right into bed."

I still hadn't said a word.

"Yes . . . that's exactly what I'll do."

As the elevator reached our floor, I pulled my hand back and shoved it deep in my pocket.

CHAPTER EIGHT

Mom's headache continued all day Monday, and on Tuesday morning she was still in bed with the shades drawn and a bag of frozen peas on her forehead.

I was just stepping out of the shower when she called out, "Can you deal with that? I don't have the—"

"Deal with what?" I asked, peeking out of the bathroom, a towel clasped around my middle.

"Someone just buzzed from downstairs . . . probably the phone company."

As Mom's voice waned, I yanked her robe off the back of the bathroom door and dashed to the intercom, slip-sliding in a trail of water along the way. After buzzing the phone company into the building, I cinched the belt around my waist, careful to check that the Grand Tetons were sufficiently swathed in terry cloth. I've worn Mom's bathrobe before and if I'm not careful, it's cleavage as far as the eye can see.

Closing the door to Mom's room, I scanned the rest of the apartment to make sure there were no bras or stray tampons lying around. When Mom and I both got our period a few mornings ago, she reminisced about how during her college days, all the girls on her hall *flowed together. Gross.* When I asked how that was possible, she launched into a description of natural scents and close proximity. *Even more gross.*

My eyes paused on the half-finished sketch clipped to a makeshift easel near the window. When we weren't hustling somewhere or another, Mom had been working on this pen-and-ink cityscape, where the layers of buildings were enunciated with streaks of charcoal.

The doorbell rang. I hugged the robe around myself, wondering if I shouldn't have thrown on some real clothes. But the phone lady didn't even end up setting foot in our apartment. She just tossed me a slip of paper with our new phone number and requested that I stick around until they were done tinkering with the cables in the basement.

As soon as she started toward the elevator, I developed an instant case of cabin fever. Not that I had anywhere to be for the next two months, but I couldn't stand the idea of being incarcerated in the apartment for an indefinite period of time. And so began the longest forty-five minutes of my life, which went something like this:

1. Pace back and forth across the room. Takes seven steps, six with longer strides.
2. Pour a bowl of cereal. Consider how this is my fourth consecutive meal of Cheerios because it's the only edible thing in the apartment, other than the no-longer-frozen peas and the staples, not exactly dream cuisine.
3. About to douse my cereal with milk when Moxie stares at me with her irresistibly *please-please-me* doggie eyes. Serve her a dish of Kibbles 'n Bits. Before I drown in self-pity for my lack of culinary variety, I remind myself that Moxie has whimperlessly stomached dog chow for seven straight years. Raise the milk carton to toast her.
4. Eat leaning against the counter, shoveling spoonfuls into my mouth. Remember how Dad used to call this a sacrilege, insisting we always sit down for meals, something about *cherishing moments.* Slurp down the remaining milk. Swipe away my lacto-mustache with the back of my hand.
5. Power up the laptop, stranded on the kitchen

table since Mom's onslaught of cover letters last week. Compose an e-mail to Kitty, giving her our new phone number. Will send as soon as the dial tone is working. Reread. Too somber, all about how New York City sucks and I wanted to cast myself off the rooftop when I called her from a pay phone and her mother said she was sailing with Jack on Cayuga Lake. Delete.

6. Peel back a Band-Aid to inspect the mama of all blisters on my heel. Slight improvement since Mom's daily walking regimen has come to a standstill, what with her impending job interviews.

7. Compose a new e-mail to Kitty, trying to sound perky and upbeat. Include an embellishment of my elevator encounter with the Johnny Depp look-alike, aka J.D. Reread. Too perky and upbeat. Delete.

8. Rinse out my cereal bowl. Omit dish soap. Feel like a rebel.

9. Pace back and forth across the room, this time lifting my knees like those Q-tip-headed guards at Buckingham Palace. *Salute. About-face.* Wonder if people know for certain when they're going bonkers, or if one day they just find themselves strapped in a straitjacket saying, *Me? But why?*

10. Compose a generic e-mail to Kitty, asking her to

call me tonight. Wish my screen name was cool like hers (hellokitty), so the next time I'm at a party and throngs of guys are sinking to their knees, begging to be my love slave, I can casually quip, "It's guitarchick at whatever dot com."

✦   ✦   ✦

"Gin!" I slammed my cards onto the kitchen table.

"Damn," Mom moaned as she fanned her cards in front of her face, "I just picked up a king."

As Mom tallied her hand, I gulped my lemonade, pausing to touch the icy glass to the back of my neck. Even though it was after seven, the apartment was feverishly hot, the exhausted old fan providing little relief.

Mom's headache finally lifted in the early evening, which is lucky, since job interview numero uno is tomorrow morning. I have to admit, I was taken aback when she rose a little while ago, her face ashen, the grooves under her eyes the shade of ripe plums.

I'd just been heading out to the corner market that's a block from our building. It's not your average convenience store with Hostess Cupcakes entombed in so much dust they would stump an archaeologist. It's stocked with soda and toilet paper, but it's also got this enormous salad bar. And I don't mean wilted iceberg lettuce, chickpeas and discolored American cheese. I'm talking gourmet cuisine—everything from sushi rolls to sliced kiwi to fried chicken, all of which you can scoop into plastic containers that they snap shut with rubber bands and weigh on the scale.

When I returned from the market, Mom was at the kitchen table, shuffling a deck of cards. Sitting in the other chair, I offered her some of my sesame noodles, but she said she wasn't hungry. Though a few minutes later, as I dealt our hands, she opened the Cheerios and began eating handfuls directly from the box. *Another Dad no-no.*

"Your turn to deal," I said, scooping up my flushes and runs and threes-of-a-kind. We were neck and neck: Mom with 71, me trailing behind with 64. The winner was the first to reach 100, so at this point it could be anyone's game.

Just then, the phone rang. A jarringly foreign sound but nonetheless music to my lonesome ears. Maybe it was Kitty! I lunged across the room.

"Hello?"

"I'm calling for Sammie," a guy's voice mumbled.

"This is Sammie."

"Hey, it's Eli."

I paused for a second, wondering how Eli got our number. Mom. She must have called Shira when I was out. I glanced at Mom, who was busily waterfalling the cards together. It makes me uncomfortable to talk on the phone when someone else is in earshot. Even though they always try to look like they're not eavesdropping, you know they are. Everyone does. You just can't help it.

"Hey." I tried to sound casual. "What's up?"

"Some friends and I are blading in Central Park on Saturday and I wanted to see if you'd like to come." Eli fired off his words without pause or intonation. Sort of a *supercalifragilisticexpialidocious* of an invitation.

The first thought that popped into my mind was that Shira put him up to this, just like the other night with the Bear Mountain episode. I can see it now. . . .

Shira: *You should bring that Sammie Davis along with you. I doubt she has a friend to her name. And with that wreck of a mother! Crying all over the salad when we were in the kitchen . . . and I'd already added salt to the dressing.*

Eli: *Awww, Mom, you don't mean LifeSavers?*

Shira: *Now, Eli . . . why don't you look at it as one of your volunteer causes? And besides, those sure didn't look like LifeSavers to me. Mountains, maybe . . .*

LifeSavers, mountains . . . I'll show them I'm not a charity case. *I am a rock. I am an aaayayayland. . . .*

"Ummm, it sounds great," I stalled, glancing at the

calendar, which I'd finally gotten around to hanging up yesterday, "but I'll be away for the Fourth of July."

Mom paused middeal. Was she in on this scheme too? Did she ask Shira to ask Eli to ask me? Why doesn't someone just lodge a bullet between my ears?

"Well, I hope you have fun," Eli said.

"Yeah . . . thanks."

There was an awkward silence.

"Okay, bye," he said.

"Bye."

"Who was that?" Mom asked as soon as I hung up.

"Eli."

"What did he want?"

"Nothing." I began sorting my hand.

"Where are you going on July fourth?"

I was on the verge of asking her if we'd stopped playing gin and started playing twenty questions, when the phone rang again. This time I let Mom get it. But as soon as I heard her ask if it was muggy in Ithaca, I flew out of my chair and grabbed the phone.

"Kitty?"

"Sammie!" she wailed. "I just got your e-mail!"

"Can you hold on for a sec?" I asked. I stretched the

phone cord into the other room and closed the door. "Okay, I'm back."

"Oh, Sammie . . . I miss you so much. You wouldn't *believe* how much has happened since you left."

I reached over to Mom's bedside table and grabbed a pencil and a scrap of paper. I always doodle when I'm on the phone, mostly while the other person is talking. Don't get me wrong; I didn't inherit a single one of Mom's artistic genes. It's nonsense stuff mostly, hearts and triangles and three-dimensional houses with bubbles of smoke billowing from the chimney. After eight years of friendship with Kitty, I bet I could cover the Sistine Chapel with my doodles, if I'd held on to them all.

It ended up being a brief conversation because Jack beeped on the other line to report that he was on his way over to pick her up. They were heading to a graduation bash and Kitty was panicked because Jack's ex would probably be there.

As Kitty described her outfit (*at once casual and sexy*), I tried to concentrate, but my mind was working a double shift. Part of me was missing Ithaca. I'd love to be getting ready for a party right now, even if I just ended up in a corner sipping lukewarm beer. At least it would be familiar. I began drawing a house. At the same time, I feel a million miles from Ithaca. To Kitty's credit, she *did* ask me about the Big (Rotten) Apple. But as soon as I began telling her about our building, she interrupted, making me promise that within the next month one of us would visit the other . . . some way, somehow.

After we hung up, I furiously scribbled window-panes and a doorknob onto my house. I felt a jumble of emotions. I guess I want to see Kitty some way, somehow. I mean, I should, shouldn't I? After all, she's my best friend. So would someone please tell me why I feel lonelier than I did before she called? I pressed the pencil so hard against the paper that the tip snapped off.

I'd just rejoined Mom at the table when the phone rang for a third time.

"I'll get it," I said, standing up. "It's probably just Kitty calling back."

"Good . . . because I've got to take something for these cramps."

As Mom headed into the bathroom, I lifted the receiver to my ear.

"Kitty?"

Silence.

I cleared my throat.

"Hello?" I asked.

"Sammie?"

Dad.

"Sammie . . . are you there?"

Oh, shit.

More silence.

More throat clearing.

"Yeah . . . ," I finally said. My throat was constricting.

"Mom gave me your number this afternoon."

"Hmmm" was all I could say. My air supply was rapidly dwindling.

"How are you?"

I considered saying, *Hurt, stranded, asphyxiating and wishing the last few months of my life had never happened,* but instead I said, "Fine."

"How's Mom?"

I considered reminding him that he'd spoken with her a few short hours ago, but instead I said, "Fine."

More silence.

Mom was flushing the toilet.

"Did you want to speak with her or something?"

"No." Dad's voice cracked. "I just wanted to make sure you're—"

"Fine," I cut him off.

"Right . . . fine."

Still more silence.

The water was running in the bathroom.

"Well, I'm going to go now," I said.

"Okay . . . fine," he said.

"Fine."

By the time I hung up, my underarms were soaking through my T-shirt. It must have been a hundred degrees in the apartment.

"Was it Kitty?" Mom asked as she dried her hands on a paper towel.

"Huh?"

"Was it Kitty . . . calling you back?"

"No." I paused. My throat was so tight it felt like I'd swallowed a whole bagel. "Wrong number."

Mom gave me a long stare. But then she flopped back in her chair, shuffled the cards and dealt herself a hand of solitaire.

CHAPTER NINE

I have a new job. It's called Elevator Duty. Here's the description: I jump on every opportunity to ride our elevator in the hopes that the automated doors will open to reveal Johnny Depp, hunk of the fifteenth floor.

I know you, he'll say, luscious lips producing a seductive half smile.

Not in the biblical sense, I'll giggle coquettishly, remembering a line I once heard on a late-night talk show.

Not yet, anyway. J.D. will wink, tickling me in that special spot above the waist, below the boobs. Kitty always says that as soon as a guy reaches for her T-spot, she knows she's got 'im, putty in her palm.

But after nearly two weeks of dressing sexy every time Moxie needed to pee, I began to worry. Maybe J.D. doesn't live in the building. Maybe meeting him was a one-time thing. Maybe he took one look at me and called his realtor, begging to move somewhere, anywhere. But then I'd remind myself how he asked if we'd "just moved in." That means he's familiar with the residents. That means he lives here. And on would go my slinky black tank top, Mom's lacy camisole, a tad of lip gloss, a spritz of vanilla musk, et cetera, et cetera.

Early Saturday morning, Moxie began circling the apartment, her nails clicking against the hardwood floor.

"Shush," I moaned, covering my eyes with one arm.

The sun was flooding through the windows, which meant that it was a little before eight, a half hour before I usually wake up. Armed with a pocketful of Baggies, I've been walking Moxie in Central Park every morning, where a beagle owner tipped me off to the policy that dogs can be off their leashes before nine A.M.

I wouldn't typically rise at the crack of dawn during summer vacation, but I've taken pity on the old girl, having to adjust from a house with a yard to two cramped rooms and millions of strange snouts sniffing every imaginable inch of her. Also, when Mom was still in her "doing NYC" phase, if I skipped out in the morning, she'd often depart without insisting I join her. Which would then grant me a few peaceful hours around the ranch, reading, playing guitar, surfing the Web. Even though Mom has now scaled back on the programming front, walking Moxie has evolved into a routine for me.

The next thing I knew, Moxie, with her *oh-so-stinky* dog breath, was panting in my face. I pushed her away. She slobbered back. We went on like that for about five minutes (*pant-pant-push-push-slobber-slobber*) until I finally lugged my tired legs onto the floor and maneuvered a bra under the T-shirt I've been sleeping in for the past several nights.

So that's how, five minutes later, I found myself trapped in the elevator with J.D., a Yankees cap on his head, baseball bat and glove in hand, grinning and asking me, "Hey, what's up?"

I began shaking like an earthquake. It wasn't supposed to happen like this, not after I've spent weeks rummaging through the apartment for any and every article of clothing with a thread of lace! And I was so busy holding my breath because I hadn't brushed my teeth that all I could do was mutely nod. I was petrified that if I cracked my lips, J.D. would:

1. Clamp his mitt over his mouth, like an oxygen mask.
2. Clobber me with his bat on grounds of stench pollution.

As soon as the door reopened, we piled out of the elevator. Me to exhale before I fainted. Moxie to gobble a biscuit from the super, who had just finished spraying down the sidewalk. J.D. to saunter toward Central Park, probably for an early game. I remained in front of the building, mesmerized by the way his butt fit into his shorts, not too snug, not too baggy, swaying as he walked.

"¿Te gusta?" the super asked me. *Do you like it?* in Spanish.

I forced my eyes away from the object of my carnal desire. The super was gesturing to the air, warm but not humid, promising a beautiful day.

"*Sí.*" I nodded. "*Me gusta.*"

"Perfect for Fourth of July."

I'd forgotten it was July fourth! The day that Eli Rosenthal and his friends were blading in Central Park. The day I told him I'd be out of town. I'm not so paranoid as to think they'd hit the park this early. But if you lie to someone about going away, you'd better make a damn good effort not to cross their path.

"Is there another place to bring dogs besides the park?"

As the super told me how to get to a dog run about

fifteen minutes away, I made a mental note to add Scope to my roster of Elevator Duty preparations.

✦ ✦ ✦

The dog run turned out to be right behind the Museum of Natural History, which is in this enormous castlelike structure that stretches along a few blocks of Central Park West. I've only been there once, when I was eight and Dad took me to see the dinosaur skeletons while Mom attended the gallery opening of a friend from art school.

As I unlatched the metal gate and started across the dog run, Moxie hung close by my side, even though I'd already taken off her leash. There were three dogs frolicking in the dirt, nipping at each other's scruff. Moxie gets intimidated in canine social situations, and I have to say, who am I to blame her? I sat down on one of the benches lining the perimeter. Moxie crouched under it, resting her head on my foot.

"Scaredy-dog?" A middle-aged man with bloodshot, droopy eyes and several chins guffawed as he pointed to Moxie, pleased as Punch about his play on words.

He was a few benches away, so I pretended I hadn't heard him as I scratched Moxie's ears.

"Dogs these days are so antisocial," Scaredy-Dog

murmured to the woman next to him, who was intently reading *The New York Times.*

Without glancing up, the woman nodded as she sipped from her tall white coffee cup. I couldn't believe Moxie was being picked on like this! Just as I was considering whether I should tell him that, a stubby little terrier, white with caramel-colored patches, tugged a girl through the gate. The girl, barely five feet tall and wearing a knee brace, attempted to restrain him. But as soon as she removed his leash, he made a beeline for Moxie, wagging his truncated tail like a hummingbird. As Moxie drew back her ears and raised the fur on her neck, I gripped her collar.

"Don't worry about him." The girl flounced down next to me. "He defies all small-dog stereotypes. He's as mellow as . . ."

As she trailed off, I quickly studied her. She was about my age, maybe a year or two younger. She was wearing a Gap T-shirt with a jog bra underneath, running shorts and sneakers. Her sandy-colored hair was pulled back from her tanned face, which was pretty, in spite of a medium case of acne.

"I can't think of anything that's mellow," she said as she reached into her backpack for a water bottle, took a swig and turned to me. "What's mellow?"

I stared at her for a second. Maybe she was thinking

of "Mellow Yellow," that old Donovan song that Dad used to listen to. I didn't say anything.

"Maybe Jell-O?" She scrunched up her nose. "No . . . Jell-O always seems so nervous, all cold and wiggly."

As her dog began rolling in the wood chips, I released my grip on Moxie's collar. That's when I noticed that the girl was hurriedly glancing back and forth between Moxie and me, shaking her head.

"I don't believe it," she gasped. Her eyes were as round as quarters. "I just don't believe it!"

"What?" I asked warily. Who was this girl, some kind of nutcase disguised as an ordinary teenager? I surveyed the dog run. Coffee Lady was fastening a harness onto her poodle, but Scaredy-Dog looked like he was settled in for the long haul. *Great.* Just the person to save my life. I can see him now, cluck-clucking his tongue, murmuring how *dogs these days* don't protect their owners.

"You are the exact same dog as your dog!"

"Huh?" I asked. Coffee Lady was opening the gate. *Now's my chance for a quick getaway.*

"You are the exact same dog as your dog," she repeated, breaking into a huge smile. "And so am I! That's very rare."

I must have given her a funny look because she quickly continued.

"I possess a sixth sense for determining what kind of

dog a person would be if they were a dog." She gulped her water, leaned toward me and whispered, "Like that man over there."

I glanced covertly at Scaredy-Dog.

"He's a basset hound."

I had to smile. Scaredy-Dog *was* the spitting image of a basset hound.

"And you're a chocolate Lab, just like your dog."

I wasn't sure whether to be offended by a complete stranger telling me I looked like my dog.

She must have read my mind because she quickly added, "It's a good thing. I'd much rather be a chocolate Lab than a Jack Russell terrier. But such are the hands we're dealt."

The girl reached into her backpack again, this time to fish out a gnarled old tennis ball. As she tossed it, her terrier scrambled away, depositing it at her feet an instant later. After a few rounds of this, Moxie lumbered over, shyly wagging her tail.

"Do you want to throw it for her?"

"No thanks. I'd probably just fling it backward."

"Not big into sports?"

"Not ones with balls," I said.

"Me neither." She giggled, throwing it all cockeyed this time, as if to exaggerate her incompetency.

When Moxie retrieved the ball, she slobbered all

over it. The girl recoiled, stretching her hand as far from her body as possible.

"Ich!"

"I'm sorry," I said. "I forgot to warn you that she's a goobermeister."

"A goobermeister!" The girl was practically in hysterics. "I'll have to remember that!"

Then she reached down and wiped her slimed hand on Moxie's shiny brown coat, adding that goobermeisters should get a taste of their own goober every now and then.

I smiled again.

"I'm Phoebe, by the way."

"And I'm Sammie."

"As in Sosa?"

"No." I paused, wrapping Moxie's leash around my hand. I hate having to explain the story behind my name, especially since the extent of the story is that my parents were spacing out. "As in Davis."

But all she said was: "Cool name! I love old Rat Pack movies."

We ended up chatting for a few more minutes as Phoebe continued throwing the ball out to the dogs. But after a while, my stomach began to rumble. I hadn't had a bite to eat yet, and I'm one of those people who wakes up with an appetite.

"I'm going to head out," I said, standing up. "It was nice to meet you."

"You too." Phoebe reached over and scratched Moxie's ears. "Just so you know, I come here every morning at nine."

"Oh."

"What's the goobermeister's name, by the way?"

"Moxie."

Phoebe grinned. "As in bold and sassy?"

"I guess." I had no clue what she was talking about, so I asked her, "What's your dog's name?"

"Dogma."

"As in principles?" We actually learned about dogma in global studies last year, one of those things that you tuck away in the back of your head, like geometry, assuming you'll never have to use it again. Dogma seems like a strange name for a terrier, but who am I to talk? My dog is named after a prescription drug.

"Bingo." Phoebe laughed. "But not as in the dog the farmer had."

This time I laughed too.

✦   ✦   ✦

Mom was still in bed when I got home. She wasn't sleeping, but she was propped against some pillows reading *Ten Days to Self-Esteem*. Not a good sign. I have this new theory that I can judge Mom's emotional state by what book she's reading. Ever since her interviews a few days ago she's been devouring the amoebas of self-help. The ones that promise insta-healing. Hundred-and-eighty-degree transformations. *Feelin' blue? Step right up 'cuz we've got the remedy!*

It's all starting to sink in, I overheard her telling Shira on the phone. After Mom announced that she'd bombed the interviews, three in a row.

When I asked Mom to clarify *bombed,* she began to cry. Something about Manhattan not being the same place she'd left fourteen years ago.

I thought about saying *Maybe you're the one who has changed, not the city.* But judging from the way her chin was quivering, I had a feeling she was thinking the same thing.

Shira had encouraged Mom to fax off thank-you notes anyway, emphasizing the high points in the interviews. But as Mom stared at the blinking cursor on the blank screen, she likened it to searching for an alpine peak in the Florida Everglades.

I collapsed on the futon. Phoebe sure was a character. I know what Kitty would've called her. *A freak.* That's how she describes anyone who doesn't *color within the lines,* as she once put it. But when I informed her that not only was I a complete failure with coloring books when I was little, but I also broke the crayons, all she said was: *Well, at least you tried. Freaks don't even try.*

I walked over to the windowsill, where I'd last sighted my dictionary. After excavating it from the bottom of a pile, I flipped through to the M's.

Moxie: 1. vigor; verve; pep. 2. courage and boldness; nerve.

How strange that no one has ever told me *moxie* is actually a real word! But then again, I never knew that every person has a dog archetype either.

Just as I was setting down the dictionary, an envelope slipped out of the back and slid to the floor. My stomach somersaulted. I didn't even have to open it to know it was that birthday card from Dad, with his California phone number.

As I held the envelope in my hand, I was tempted to pick up the phone and dial the eleven digits. Right here. Right now.

Maybe I'd tell Dad that I'm not as fine as I say every time he asks.

Or maybe I'd let him know that, despite everything, I miss spending time together, miss having a father.

Or maybe I'd just say *Hey, Jimmy D., what's new?* like it was any other day.

But I couldn't.

Instead, I shoved the card back into the dictionary, stormed over to the mirror and studied my reflection. So maybe Moxie and I both have chestnut-colored hair. And I guess we have similar puppyish brown eyes. But only one of us is "bold and sassy," and I'll tell you right now that it's not me.

CHAPTER TEN

When the phone rang on Tuesday afternoon, I'd been tooling around the apartment, feeling sort of useless. Daytime television, I've now decided, caters to people with an IQ in the single digits. And if you weren't a Neanderthal to start out with, it gobbles up your brain cells quicker than a tank of vodka. But, of course, you park there, eyes fixed on the tube, thinking, *This is truly rubbish; maybe I'll watch for seventeen more hours.*

Mom had gone to Long Island for the day to visit her older brother, the one who called her Onion when she was little. His name is Steve and he's a high-powered businessman, constantly flashing his cell phone, Palm Pilot, corporate credit cards. And even though he has enough frequent-flier miles to jet to the moon, he's always remarking how Ithaca isn't exactly a *key destination*. Thus we're forced to pack up and visit him once a year. Dad was usually cool with it, feigning a weekend interest in digital gadgets or Aunt Mimi's new-but-never-used kitchen. And thanks to their mega-solar dish, I would see it as an opportunity to catch up on my Japanese soaps. But three days at Uncle Steve's never failed to leave Mom with hives, a pounding headache, a nervous tic or some combination of the three.

If I were feeling compassionate, I'd say Uncle Steve has a short fuse. But if I were being completely honest, I'd say he's a jerk. For example, when Mom was applying to art school, Uncle Steve told her she'd be better off flushing her money down the toilet. And since he'd taken charge of the finances after their father had died, he refused to give her a penny. Luckily Mom received scholarships, but she worked herself to the bone waiting tables to cover room and board. Mom calls him strict. I call him the Original Asshole, but only to myself.

Dad once explained to me that Mom continues reaching out to her brother to heal the wounds from her childhood. Supposedly, after her father collapsed from a heart attack at the age of forty-five, her mother closed up shop, aging decades overnight. Whenever I think about a thirteen-year-old Mom being left to raise herself, I feel sad. I feel sympathetic. But I don't feel any fonder toward the Original Asshole.

So when Mom gave me the option of joining her today, I decided to pass. And better I did because Mom called from Penn Station to report that not only had she missed her train, but she'd forgotten her address book and Uncle Steve's number was unlisted, so would I let them know she'd be on the ten-forty instead? Which meant I had to chitchat with Aunt Mimi, who is so self-involved that even Mom laughed when I joked that her name should be changed to Me-Me.

The phone didn't ring again until afternoon, while I was struggling to thread a new D-string on my guitar. Dad had showed me how to change the strings after they snap, but it's still a task to tune them.

"Hello?"

"Roz?"

It was Shira.

"No, it's Sammie."

"You sound exactly like your mother."

I glanced at my fingers. I've been playing guitar so much recently that I'm developing calluses on the fingertips of my left hand.

"Is she around?"

"No. She's visiting my uncle for the day."

"Damn."

"Is everything okay?"

"I'm actually having a little crisis. I'm stuck in a meeting for at least another hour and I'm supposed to pick up Becca from gymnastics at four o'clock. I can't reach Eli at the gardens, so I was hoping Roz could run over there and—"

"I can do it."

"Really?" Shira paused. "It's all the way on the Upper East Side. Do you know how to get there?"

"I've taken the crosstown bus a few times. I'll make it."

As Shira rattled off directions, I rummaged through my backpack for quarters, since Mom had taken the MetroCard with her.

"Oh, Sammie, I don't know how to thank you." Shira breathed a long sigh of relief. "You really are a life-saver."

I was glad Eli wasn't in the background to hear *that* one.

✦   ✦   ✦

Becca did a double take when she waltzed out of gymnastics and I was waiting there, a little flushed from having racewalked fifteen blocks because I'd forgotten to ask the driver for a transfer to the uptown bus. The whole transit system still feels confusing, even with the maps I picked up in the subway station. Especially since the only bus I'd taken up until this summer was a banana-yellow school bus.

It was such a beautiful afternoon that Becca and I decided to walk home. The sun was shining, my blisters were nearly gone and, I have to say, it was a relief to hear someone else's voice, to get my mind off things. It's been almost a week since Mom's bombed interviews. And since she hasn't heard a peep from any of them, she's convinced that she's utterly unemployable in today's market. Whenever I think about it, I launch into a full-scale anxiety attack. Especially at night, when I lie in bed, feeling like I'll never be able to take another deep breath.

But as Becca and I walked across Central Park, I actually could have passed for a relaxed human being. It was only as we rode up in the elevator that I tensed up again. What if Eli is home from the gardens already? I still feel weird that I lied to him about the Fourth of July. Mom promised to cover for me when she grabbed Indian food with Shira a few nights ago. I was actually pretty surprised, seeing that she was the one who brought it up.

You know I'm the Abe Lincoln of honesty, Mom said as

she twisted her hair into a comb on the back of her head. *But if Shira asks, I'll say you had plans with a friend.*

The Rosenthals' apartment turned out to be empty and silent. Part of me felt disappointed, though I can't explain why. It's like I'd somehow been looking forward to all hell breaking loose as I blundered over my words when Eli asked where I'd gone last weekend. Which is much more Kitty Lundquist than Sammie Davis. Kitty lives in a soap opera, complete with lust and betrayal and seven simultaneous subplots. I tend toward the Sunday Night Disney Movie: practical, predictable, pathetically G-rated.

As I lingered in the foyer, Becca bounded into the kitchen. "Cherry or grape?"

I wasn't sure what she was talking about so I just said, "Whatever you're having."

Becca reappeared with two purple Popsicles. As she handed one to me, she exclaimed, "I have to say, I like you a lot more than Jenna!"

"Jenna?"

"Oops." Becca began slurping at her Popsicle. "I've said too much already. Eli would murder me if he knew I—"

Becca clamped her hand over her violet-stained lips, leaving me bursting with curiosity. *Who is Jenna? And why can't Becca tell me about her?* Damn! Kitty would know just how to girl-talk Becca, to initiate a giggly bonding session until all the secrets spilled out. I, on the other hand, shrugged as nonchalantly as possible, in a fabricated attempt at *I couldn't care less.*

We'd been home for about a half hour when Shira flew through the door, toting two grocery bags and a long, slim baguette wrapped in white paper. Kicking off her sandals, she headed for the kitchen. Becca and I trailed after her.

"Thank you so much, Sammie." Shira hauled a gallon of milk into the fridge.

"No problem."

I leaned against the counter. Becca climbed onto a tall stool.

"Tuesdays are always my hard day," Shira explained as she unpacked the groceries. "I have an all-staff meeting downtown. One of those things I just can't get out of."

"I can pick up Becca next week too, if you want."

"Yes, yes, yes, yes, yes!" Becca sprang off her stool and began jumping up and down.

Shira laughed. "I know someone who'd like that."

"Yes, yes, yes, yes, yes!"

"Of course, I'd pay you to do it."

"You don't have to." I began fiddling with a rubber band that had been on the counter.

Shira rooted through her shoulder bag. As she held some bills in my direction, I tried not to look at them, but I think I glimpsed a five and a bunch of ones.

"I insist." Shira pressed the money into my hand.

"Thanks."

"Thank *you*." Shira paused. "Would you like to stay for dinner, by the way?"

"Yes, yes, yes, yes, yes!" Becca cried.

"Ummm, I—I . . . ," I stammered.

"It's not going to be much, just some leftover gazpacho," Shira said, "and Eli is having dinner at a friend's."

The rubber band snapped out of my hand, flew across the kitchen and struck a low cupboard. I shot a glance at Shira. Does she think I don't want to see Eli? Or maybe he doesn't want to see *me*? Or maybe this has something to do with Jenna. . . .

"So we need to fill our teenager quota," Shira added.

Becca's eyes darted back and forth between Shira and me.

"Okay," I finally said, "sure."

"Great." Shira smiled. "You can make the salad."

As I broke apart leaves of romaine lettuce, Shira shepherded Becca into the shower. I kept thinking about this time, three or four years ago, when Mom had made gazpacho. It's a chilled Spanish soup that's perfect on hot days. By mistake, I'd asked for a second helping of *gestapo,* which made Mom and Dad laugh so hard they'd almost choked on their iced coffees. Dad had finally explained that the gestapo were the German secret police during the Nazi regime, notorious for their brutality. *Right continent, at least,* Mom had added, wiping her eyes.

"Everything okay in here?" Shira asked as she reappeared in the kitchen.

"Yeah, fine."

Shira began slicing the baguette onto a wooden cutting board. As I rinsed the lettuce, I placed the clean leaves in the strainer she'd given me.

"How are things going, Sammie?"

I froze, letting the chilly water trickle over my fingers.

"What do you mean?"

Shira rested the bread knife in the middle of the loaf.

"I know this is a particularly hard time for Roz right now." She paused. "All these changes." She paused again. "I just wanted to see how you're coping with things."

My face scrunched up like I was going to bawl. I don't get this feeling very often, but when I do, I know exactly what it is. *Five more seconds and I'm a goner.*

"You may be okay," Shira quickly added. "I don't want to . . ."

As her voice trailed off, I swallowed several times and repeated to myself: *Control, control, control, control, control.*

"Yeah, I'm okay," I finally mumbled. Then I diverted my attention to a clump of dirt, scrubbing as if my life depended upon its removal.

After a second, I gulped in some air, turned to Shira and said, more confidently this time: "Really I am."

"Glad to hear it." Shira reached over and tousled my hair, in such a motherly way that the tears instantly piled up behind my eyes again. I turned back to the lettuce. *This is going to be the most pristine fucking salad in the whole world.*

Shira resumed slicing the bread. "But if you ever need someone to talk to—"

"Thanks."

My fingers had grown so cold from the water that they were practically numb. When I ran them under the hot tap, the blood rushed in so quickly it made them ache. But I caught myself before I cried out, biting my lip instead.

CHAPTER ELEVEN

When Mom returned from Long Island, her neck and stomach were covered in red blotchy hives.

"Uncle Steve was worse than ever," Mom said, unbuttoning her blouse and standing in front of the oscillating fan. Mom always dresses up to see the Original Asshole, like the middle-aged version of a "good girl." And today she'd come through in spades: a pressed white blouse, a beige linen skirt (below the knees, of course), pumps. Yes, real, honest-to-goodness canoe shoes! The last time Mom had worn pumps was to her coworker's son's bar mitzvah two years ago and on the car ride home she'd had Dad pull up next to a Dumpster so she could toss them in.

I didn't respond. I was busy hanging a new poster

above the futon. Mom had said it would be okay, as long as I used thumbtacks. Well, it's not new exactly. More vintage. I bought it at a used-book-and-record shop on upper Broadway. It's an old placard from the 1965 Newport Folk Festival, where Bob Dylan notoriously plugged in an electric guitar. Some say it changed the course of music. I just like looking at the names of all the folkie legends like Pete Seeger and Joan Baez.

"He laid into me about uprooting you from Ithaca, bringing you to the city."

I glanced at Mom.

"Do you feel uprooted?"

I shrugged. I really didn't feel like having this conversation right now.

"And get this." Mom began running a washcloth under the tap. "As we were driving to the train station in his brand-new Lexus, he took it upon himself to stress that he won't bail me out, you know, financially."

Mom was wringing the washcloth like she wished it was the Original Asshole's neck.

"As if I'd ever ask him." She sighed.

I studied the poster. I'd hung it pretty crooked, with the left side at least an inch higher than the right. I should probably do it over. But not now. Now, I just wanted to split before Mom started up about money again. She'd nearly had a breakdown yesterday morning, as she attempted to balance her dwindling checkbook, a stack of unpaid bills at her side.

"Remind me how difficult he is the next time I get the bright idea to go out there." Mom blotted the washcloth against her bare neck and stomach.

"Gladly," I said, and then I grabbed my keys and headed up to the roof.

✦ ✦ ✦

On Friday, Mom's forty-third birthday rolled around. She'd been saying all week that she wanted to low-key it, that she wasn't up for a big celebration. But it still seemed like she needed something to snap her out of the malaise that has descended over the past few weeks. I'd already trekked back to the boutique where she'd gotten that vanilla spray and purchased an assortment of fruit-scented soaps. But the real present I was saving for dinnertime.

I spent the morning scouring *Moosewood*, the bible of vegetarian cookbooks. Moosewood Restaurant— located in none other than downtown Ithaca—is Mom's favorite place to eat. Since Dad and I used to take her there for her birthday every summer, I decided to recreate the granola-lovin' café right in our apartment.

I had to hit three different grocery stores to find all the ingredients for Balkan cucumber salad, eggplant curry with basmati rice and, for dessert, homemade berry sorbet, which I would mix right in our blender. And just before I reached the cashier at the second place, I tossed a box of plastic straws into my shopping basket. I can't remember if Moosewood is too eco-psycho to use straws, but I thought it would give it more of a restauranty feel.

As I chopped and peeled and sautéed and spiced away the afternoon, I made Mom steer clear of the kitchen. I even served her a glass of iced coffee and a plateful of Oreos when she said something about being hungry. So by the time dinner rolled around, as I led her to the table blindfolded by my hand, I'd successfully concealed the Moosewood theme.

"Ta-da," I sang, steering her into her chair. "Happy birthday!"

"Wow," Mom said as she surveyed the spread. I noticed her eyes resting on the sheet of loose-leaf paper that I'd tacked above the table, with the words Moosewood Restaurant scrawled in neon-pink highlighter, the only marker I'd been able to find for my last-minute inspiration.

I hovered above her chair, grinning expectantly.

"Wow," Mom said again, with even less gusto than the last time.

I didn't want her lack of enthusiasm to get to me. But after fifteen minutes of me declaring how sumptuous the food was, exaggeratedly wiping my lips with a (ah-hem) cloth napkin and generously helping myself to seconds of everything, I began to worry. Mom had eaten about three bites of the salad, and besides picking out a few fresh peas, she hadn't even touched the eggplant dish.

I set down my fork.

"It's delicious, Sammie." Mom nibbled at a walnut. "Really it is."

I tried not to let my lower lip protrude too much.

Mom began rearranging the food on her plate. "I'm just not that hungry tonight . . . you know . . . the hives . . ."

As Mom's voice trailed off, I noticed her looking past me, over my shoulder. I followed her gaze to my Newport poster, which I'd finally gotten around to straightening this morning.

"The first year Dad and I were together, we went to hear Pete Seeger and Arlo Guthrie play at Carnegie Hall." She pushed around her rice until it formed an O, like a doughnut. "Dad was so wired when we back to our apartment that he stayed up half the night playing protest songs on his guitar."

I glanced across the room at my guitar case propped against the wall. My mouth suddenly felt dry. I sipped at the fresh-squeezed lemonade until there was nothing left but ice cubes, and then I began grinding the straw between my incisors.

"He played all of them . . . 'If I Had a Hammer,' 'We Shall Overcome,' 'Where Have All the Flowers Gone?' " The corners of Mom's lips were turned up in a faint smile. "Vietnam was long gone by then, but if you took one look at him that night, you never would have guessed it—"

And then Mom choked up. I looked away.

"I'm sorry." Mom shook her head as she swabbed the rivulet of tears rolling down her cheeks. "You made a beautiful dinner, Sammie . . . I'm so sorry . . . I just need to lie down for a bit."

Mom headed toward the bathroom. A second later, I heard the tub running. I got up and closed the door between our rooms.

When I turned and caught sight of the table, the sign, the beeswax candle I'd forgotten to light, I felt nauseous.

Nice try, kid. Fooling yourself into thinking a little food could make it all go away.

After a half hour or so, Mom switched out her light. I can always tell because the strip under the door goes black. I reached over and picked up the phone. I've dialed Kitty's number so many times I can do it with my eyes closed.

Kitty answered on the third ring.

"Hello?"

"Hi," I said, not even trying to keep the edge out of my voice.

"Sammie . . . I was about to call you," she moaned, "I'm so upset. . . ."

"Why?"

"Remember how Jack wanted to spice up our sex life?"

"Yeah."

"Well, I have a hunch he's been shopping on another spice rack."

"What are you talking about?"

"I think he's having an affair," Kitty said flatly.

"Are you serious?"

"He's been, quote, busy the past three nights, and I pulled up next to his ex at a traffic intersection yesterday and she gave me a funny look."

"Did you ask him?"

"No," Kitty whimpered, "he's always saying how trust is essential to a relationship."

I should become a therapist. I swear, I wouldn't have to do one thing differently and I'd make a bundle more than as a baby-sitter. Except I'd really needed someone to listen to me tonight, to reassure me that I hadn't fucked up.

As Kitty blew her nose, I considered telling her just that. But that's when she said something that piqued my interest.

"You know those people who sublet your house?"

"Sure . . . the Oscar Mayer Wieners."

"Call them that all you want," she sniffled, "but they have a daughter our age who's totally gorgeous."

"A daughter?" Up until that moment, I'd maintained my illusion of the son, the farm boy, the monkey-spanker.

"Every guy in Ithaca wants to ask her out."

Hearing that was the final straw. I lived in that damn house for fourteen celibate years and this girl is in town for what? A few weeks? And she's already the hit of the social scene? If I were a camel, I'd be in a body cast right now because my back would be broken.

CHAPTER TWELVE

Phoebe was the only one in the dog run when I arrived the next morning. I spotted her from half a block away, sitting on a bench with Dogma on her lap.

"Sammie and Goobermeister!" Phoebe shouted, waving. "I was hoping you'd come back."

I lingered near the gate while Moxie galloped over to Phoebe. As Dogma hopped onto the ground, Phoebe slid over on the bench, patting the empty spot next to her.

"Are you trying to goober up my tennis ball again?" Phoebe asked Moxie, who was nosing at her backpack.

Joining Phoebe, I noticed she still had that brace on her knee. I bet she's torn a ligament or something.

"How was your week?" Phoebe asked, tossing the tennis ball across the dog run.

I shrugged.

"Not so good?"

I shook my head as I fiddled with the metal gadget on Moxie's leash.

"Me neither."

"Why not?"

"I asked you first," Phoebe said.

I paused. Part of me was tempted to spill the emotional beans, like those tell-all families on daytime talk shows who curse, throw chairs at each other and eventually make up. I wondered how Phoebe would react if I told her about Dad taking off for California without me. Or the fact that Mom had been curled in the fetal position under her sheets when I'd left the apartment a few minutes ago.

"I just moved here this summer," I finally said, "so I don't really know anyone in the city."

"Really? Where did you move from?"

"Ithaca. It's a town in central New—"

"I know where Ithaca is! My older sister went to Cornell."

"Really?" I couldn't believe it! Maybe she'd even taken a class with Dad. Supposedly his American lit class was so popular that undergrads audited lectures *just for fun,* a notion that always struck me as bizarre.

"She went to the vet school, but now she lives in Tucson. Guess what she specializes in."

My mind flashed to Oscar Mayer Wienermom, who I remembered was going to work at the vet school. Which then led me to Oscar Mayer Wienerette and the droves of guys lining up at *my* front door. I can see it now, with them saying, *Who lived here, again? Samantha who? Never heard of her.*

"Dogs," Phoebe continued. "We're a big dog family."

I glanced over to where Moxie and Dogma were digging a hole.

"I mean, we're big *into* dogs, but the only dogs we've ever had are *small* ones."

I had to laugh.

"By the way, now you know one person in New York City."

Just then Dogma bounded over and leaped back into Phoebe's lap, smudging dirt all over her legs.

"And one dog," she added.

Phoebe didn't tell me about *her* bad week until we were in Riverside Park, where she suggested we go after the dog run was invaded by three snarling boxers and a springer spaniel. Or at least that was the type of dog that Phoebe deemed the guy who corralled them in on a web of knotted ropes.

Riverside Park turned out to be on a narrow stretch

of land bordering the Hudson River, overflowing with families, mutts and little kids teetering on their bikes. I could have ridden Mariposa here, if I'd been able to bring her. As Phoebe and I walked up the promenade, I discovered I'd been wrong about her on two counts:

1. She's going to be seventeen in September, so she's nearly a year older than I am. I must have looked surprised because she laughed and said, *Don't worry, people always assume I'm younger because I'm such a runt.*

2. Her knee wasn't injured, as she confessed during part of *her* bad-week story, which went something like this: Earlier this summer her parents had sent her to a six-week tennis camp where her older siblings had thrived, even though she hates the sport. But three days in, opportunity knocked when she tripped on a tree root and twisted her knee. The sports doctor banned her from the courts. The camp offered to reimburse tuition. Phoebe hopped the next bus home. But now her parents are saying she has to return when her knee heals, so Phoebe is faking a limp whenever she's in their presence.

Phoebe was still walking fine by lunchtime, when we bought hot dogs from a street vendor. As we dangled our feet over the river, Moxie begged for a scrap of my food.

"It really *is* a dog-eat-dog world." Phoebe giggled.

Phoebe was always making dog references, every opportunity she could get. Like when we were throwing our wrappers into a trash bin, she pointed to a woman jogging by us, with a sturdy build and strawberry blond hair.

"What do you think she is?"

"A golden retriever?" I whispered.

"Not bad." Phoebe wiped some relish off her cheek. "A *Chesapeake Bay* retriever."

Phoebe also pointed out cute guys. "I'm the first to admit I'm boy-crazy!" she exclaimed as we passed a schoolyard where some guys were playing three-on-three basketball.

"Mmmm," she moaned as one of them ripped off his shirt, exposing a six-pack stomach, "I like my men built."

I stepped back a little so it wasn't obvious we were watching them. I wonder how much experience Phoebe has, if she's more like Kitty or more like me. If I had to guess, I'd say she's somewhere in between.

By late afternoon, we found ourselves back at the metal gate outside the dog run.

"Well." Phoebe gestured toward Columbus Avenue. "I go up here."

"And I go down."

We stood there for a second. Dogma began whining and tugging at his leash.

"Hope to see you soon," Phoebe said.

"Me too."

We'd just started off in opposite directions when Phoebe called out, "Sammie?"

"Yeah?" I turned around.

Phoebe grinned. "I had a dog-day afternoon."

"Me too," I said again, smiling this time.

But when I entered our apartment a few minutes later, I got a queasy feeling. It was stuffy and still and exactly the way I'd left it in the morning, with my bowl on the counter, two pillows situated on either end of the futon and my sorry-ass Moosewood sign crumpled on top of a stack of newspapers ready to go out for recycling. Directly within my eyeshot was Mom's pen-and-ink sketch, still clipped to the easel, untouched now for several weeks. It was strange to look at the half-finished cityscape, with windowless buildings and partially erected skyscrapers. Almost as if the contractors had pricked their fingers on a cursed spinning wheel and fallen into a deep slumber for a hundred years.

My gut told me to go right back outside again, but my bladder insisted I had to pee. Phoebe had fast-talked her way into a diner a little while ago, but I always feel weird about doing that, especially when there's a sign posted on the door that says Rest Room for Customers Only.

When I peeked into Mom's room, my fears were confirmed. The blinds were drawn and Mom was sprawled on her stomach with her bare legs twisted in a tangle of sheets. While I was tiptoeing out of the bathroom, she glanced at me through a veil of matted hair.

"Are you okay?" I whispered. "Do you have another headache?"

Mom shook her head, but I wasn't sure if that meant no, she wasn't okay or no, she didn't have a migraine.

"Can I get you anything? A glass of water?"

"That'd be great." Mom's voice was barely audible, what with her face burrowed in a mound of pillows.

I twisted some ice cubes out of the tray and plunked them into a tall glass. I couldn't get this unsettling thought out of my mind: What if Dad suddenly attributed the trial separation to a temporary brain lapse and rolled into town, intent on nestling back into connubial bliss? I bet if he saw Mom like this he'd run for them thar hills. Sprint would be more like it.

As I took her the water, I decided that I should do everything within my power to keep things around the apartment as normal as possible. Because if I didn't, who would?

C H A P T E R T H I R T E E N

Over the next few weeks, I was in a near-constant state of anxiety, to a point where it was normal for my throat to be tight, my cheeks tense, my breath hard to catch. At night I would fall into bed, my body zapped of energy, and dream about separating lights from darks in the laundry room and ATM machines running out of cash. There was just so much to remember that my brain felt like our wearied old fan, whirring night and day in a cycle like this:

1. Is there anything to eat in the apartment? Answer is often no, which means I have to make a shopping list and trek to several grocery stores in an attempt to hit all the sales advertised in the windows.

2. Has Moxie been fed and walked? And why does she keep gnawing that raw patch on her back?

3. Is today a day I have to remind Mom about alternate-side parking? And what if another episode like last Thursday happens? I hadn't been able to rouse her in time, so as the street cleaners advanced, I'd grabbed her car keys and begged the super to move the Volvo while I hyperventilated from the sidewalk.

The only times my mind slows down are when I'm playing guitar or hanging out with Phoebe. We've been meeting in the dog run every morning. Sometimes we just sit on a bench, chatting as Moxie and Dogma horse around. Other times we wander around Central Park for hours, until Phoebe "limps" off to physical therapy.

I guess I'd say we're becoming friends. It's strange. We haven't exchanged phone numbers and I still don't even know her last name. And it's not like we make plans to meet; we both just show up at the dog run at nine, an unspoken agreement. In a way, the fact that we're completely unattached allows us to talk about things you ordinarily don't when you've just met some-one.

Like on Friday afternoon, as we were walking around the reservoir, Phoebe told me that after her release from tennis captivity, she'd assumed it was going to be a lonely summer. Most of her friends were counselors at sleep-away camps, or with their families out in the Hamptons, which she described as these swank beach towns near the eastern tip of Long Island.

"If you can call them friends," she added, scuffing her sneakers in the pebbles.

"What do you mean?"

And that's when Phoebe told me about her stuffy private school, where the kids believe that a hefty allowance + designer clothes + a country home = high status. Phoebe's parents often forgo vacations to cover tuition because they believe that education equals enlightenment. What they don't understand is that all the teachers talk about is how education equals good college applications.

"Can't you tell them you want to transfer somewhere else?" I asked.

And that's when Phoebe told me how her older siblings, both in their midtwenties, had gone there too. And how her sister had excelled at Cornell; her brother was a nuclear physicist "with more degrees than a thermometer." And how her parents pressure her to live up to that precedent, not realizing that to the rest of the world these wunderkinder aren't exactly normal.

The next morning, while we were sitting on a pier in Riverside Park, I told Phoebe that I understand what it's like to live in someone else's shadow.

"What do you mean?" she asked.

And that's when I described Kitty. How she has the brains and the beauty and the boys. How I once compiled a list of all of Kitty's assets (seventeen) and all of mine (two), which I then shredded into pieces and stuffed in the trash. And how, next to Kitty, I often wind up feeling second-tier.

Phoebe's eyes had been closed as she aimed her face toward the sun. I think she was trying to dry up her acne, which has gotten worse over the past few weeks.

"Sammie." She sat up abruptly and looked at me. "You are *anything* but second-tier."

It could have just been the sun making its way over the Manhattan skyline, but I was suddenly overcome with a warm sensation inside. I knew that, whether or not it was actually true, Phoebe meant what she said.

I got a similar feeling a few days later, when I showed up at the dog run racked with a lousy, crampy, moody case of PMS.

"You need chocolate," Phoebe said matter-of-factly.

But when we scavenged around in our pockets, we didn't have enough collectively to buy a Hershey's Kiss.

I was about to succumb to premenstrual funk when Phoebe marched me down the street to this chichi-froufrou chocolate shop, where truffles are worth their weight in gold. After tying Moxie and Dogma to a parking meter, Phoebe dragged me past displays of delicately wrapped gourmet chocolates, ignoring my hushed reminders of our penniless state.

"My friend and I are regular customers here"— Phoebe smiled at the person behind the counter, a petite woman with closely set dark eyes and cascades of long reddish hair framing her fragile face—"and we wanted to see what you're sampling today."

Regular customers here? What if she takes one look and says she's never seen us before in her life? I was debating whether I should flee the scene of the crime or defend Phoebe on grounds of PMS prevention when the saleswoman said, "We're sampling our new line of milk chocolate hazelnuts. Does that sound okay to you?"

Okay to us? I considered asking her if she'd ever heard the expression "Beggars can't be choosers," when she selected two morsels from a nearby tray. She was even shorter than Phoebe, who is exactly five feet tall, so she had to stand on her tippy-toes to pass them over the high counter.

"Thanks," I mumbled, tearing off the crinkly brown

foil. It was creamy and delicious and vanished in one pop.

"Mmm," Phoebe said, "thank you."

Once we were out on the street, Phoebe opened her fist and revealed her chocolate, still in its wrapping.

"Just what the doctor ordered," she pronounced, handing it to me.

"No." I attempted to give the chocolate back to her. "It's yours."

But Phoebe held both her hands in the air, refusing to take it. Then she paused, deliberately scratched her temple and giggled. "A shih tzu, don't you think?"

"What?"

Phoebe gestured toward the woman in the shop. "Those little dogs with the long, long fur."

"Oh," I tried to say, but my mouth was full of milk chocolate hazelnut. Even though they came from the exact same tray, I could swear this one tasted even better than the first.

✦　✦　✦

There *are* things I didn't tell Phoebe. I didn't tell her that my parents had separated so recently. And I didn't tell her that Dad had suddenly decided I was no longer his Number One Daughter, like he always used to joke, pshawing away my reminder that I was his Number

Only Daughter. And I didn't tell her how many hours Mom sits at the kitchen table playing solitaire or flipping through her selection of self-help books. And I definitely didn't tell her about Dad's phone call the following week.

It had caught me off guard, in a rare moment when I was home alone. I'd just finished washing Moxie with a dog shampoo that Phoebe's sister, Charlotte, had recommended to reduce itching. Phoebe had e-mailed her in Tucson, after the patch on Moxie's back grew raw and flaky.

I tossed a towel over Moxie's damp fur, closed her in the bathroom and dove toward the receiver, answering on the third ring. My T-shirt was sopping wet and my arms felt slimy from the suds.

It turned out to be Dad, with his usual *How are you? How's Mom? Are you sure?* and me with my *Fine, Fine, Yes, I'm sure.* I examined a blunt scratch on my thigh, most likely from Moxie's attempted escape during the rinse-off. I couldn't believe how calm I felt. I could almost get used to this.

"In case you try to reach me," Dad said right before we hung up, "Aunt Jayne and I are taking a cycling trip down the coast in two weeks."

I sank onto the futon, even though my shorts were relatively damp. That was *my* plan with Dad, before all the trial separation business! I was going to bring Mariposa to Palo Alto, and if we were in good enough shape by the end of the summer, we were going to cycle as far as Los Angeles and then fly back with our bikes.

I hadn't realized I was so replaceable, I thought about saying. But I didn't. I barely said another word until we got off the phone a few minutes later.

After we hung up, I thought of that Dr. Seuss book, *Horton Hatches the Egg.* It's about how Mayzie the Lazy Bird convinces an elephant to tend to her egg while she flits off to Palm Beach, and then demands it back once it's about to hatch. When I was four, I used to make Dad read it to me every night, even though I'd memorized it so completely I would stop him if he altered even a word.

I scratched my arm. The soap was beginning to irritate my skin. I could hear Moxie whimpering from behind the door. As I headed toward the bathroom, I wondered what would happen if Dad ever stopped his lazy-bird act and decided to become a father again. I couldn't say whether I let him back into the nest again. After all, *Horton* ends up gaining custody of the offspring, *not* Mayzie the Lazy Bird.

✦   ✦   ✦

I *did* tell Phoebe about Kitty's panicky phone call two days later. Well, I tried to, at least. Because I hadn't even gotten to the part where Kitty discovered con-doms in the glove compartment of Jack's Jeep even though she'd gone on the Pill two months ago, when Phoebe sucked in her breath.

"Your best friend has had SEX?"

"Yeah." I nodded, glancing around the dog run. Phoebe had said that so loudly I wouldn't be surprised if the people walking down Columbus had heard it. In fact, I wouldn't be surprised if Kitty had heard it all the way in Ithaca. I wonder how she'd feel if she knew I told Phoebe about her, about Jack. For some reason, I'd rather not think about that.

I should have guessed Phoebe's next question.

"Have you?"

I shook my head. "Not even close."

Phoebe exhaled, her shoulders sagging. "Me nei-ther."

We were quiet for a minute. I have to admit, I'm glad Phoebe is still a virgin. It makes me feel more normal somehow. I wonder if she's done other things, like sec-ond base or even third.

"Have you done anything else?" she asked.

I began to describe the Big Slobbery Makeout at sail-ing camp last summer. I told her how his tongue felt like a giant wet worm invading my mouth. And how strange it was, when you can barely swap chewing gum with your closest friend, to have a stranger's spit sliding down your chin. It wasn't until I recounted how he pushed his pointy bulge against my thigh that I realized Phoebe had been digging her fingernails into my wrist.

"You're so lucky," she sighed as soon as I'd finished.

And that's when she confessed that she hasn't done anything yet, not even a peck. That the closest she's come is a cyber-boyfriend she met in a teen chat room. His screen name is Mountainking. They e-mail every day and have even scanned photos back and forth, but it's a long way from New York to Denver.

"And it's not for lack of knowledge," Phoebe added wistfully.

"What do you mean?"

"I know everything there is to know about sex . . . without having done a thing."

"How?"

"I've read tons of books on human sexuality and my sister, Charlotte, is my direct pipeline to the practical side."

"The hands-on," I cut in.

"Good one," Phoebe giggled, and then began describing an online sex advice column she wants to write someday. She'd call it "Frank Talk," since her last name is Frank.

I was about to tell her that I hadn't known her last name was Frank, that it was perfectly suited to her, when she gripped my wrist, this time with both her hands.

"Sammie?" she asked, a grin creeping over her face.

"Yeah?"

"Will you tell me about the Big Slobbery Makeout one more time?"

Maybe it was all the sex talk, but good karma descended around noon, as I was on my way home. I almost missed it altogether because as I rounded our corner, I'd been trying to decide whether to make a grilled cheese sandwich or a tuna melt for lunch.

It took me a minute to realize someone was honking their horn, trying to get my attention. I glanced over just in time to catch J.D. saluting as he revved up a silver Honda and peeled down the block.

Maybe we'll drive off like that together someday, on our way to a weekend retreat in the Hamptons. I'll buckle my seat belt as the tires screech when the car whips around the corner.

Sammie, you know you're safe with me, he'll murmur, squeezing my leg right above the knee.

Let's say I don't want to be safe anymore, I'll giggle as his hand wanders up my thigh.

Once we get to the ocean, we'll find a small deserted

beach shaded by trees. I'll wear a two-piece bathing suit, and I won't obsess about the stretch marks on my thighs or my Grand Tetons. And as we slip into the warm, salty water, my mind will not be on Mom, Dad or alternate-side parking. No, all I'll think about will be the sun on my shoulders, the sand between my toes and J.D.'s fingers untying my bikini top.

CHAPTER FOURTEEN

The heat wave started on the last Tuesday of July. By eight in the morning, the sun was piercing the windows and radio broadcasters were warning that physical activity should be limited due to poor air quality. Phoebe and I had only been in the dog run for twenty minutes when Dogma flopped onto his side with his eyes drooping. She scooped him up and carried him home, exaggerating her limp as she turned onto Columbus. And as I headed in the other direction, the sun charring my shoulders, Moxie was panting so badly that a waiter at an outdoor café poured her a bowl of water.

The worst thing of all was our apartment. Mom had given me her credit card to buy another fan the week before, when the temperature hit ninety. But by noon, as the radio reported the heat index in the three-digit range, the fans were providing as much relief as a parakeet fluttering its wings in the Sahara Desert. As Mom stepped into her second cool shower, I collapsed on the futon, fully sympathizing with the cry of a lobster when chucked into a pot of boiling water. By late afternoon, Mom agreed to check with the super about an air conditioner. But I was running out the door to pick up Becca from gymnastics, so I didn't stick around to see if she'd follow through.

I've been watching Becca for the past three Tuesdays. Shira always insists I stay for dinner, which is fine. And she's never again pulled me aside to query my emotional state. Though last week, as I was scraping plates while she stacked them in the dishwasher, I considered saying something about feeling overwhelmed by Mom, by tending to our lives. I never even told anyone about my first-ever outbreak of hives. I'd just borrowed some of Mom's lotion and kept my mouth shut. But just as I was gearing up to talk to Shira, Becca teetered into the kitchen with an armload of dishes and the moment was gone.

Anyway, I have a hunch Shira already knows Mom's not doing that well. She calls every evening to check up on her and they meet for coffee at least once a week.

Whenever Mom returns from spending time with Shira, she always seems a little less blue. Which is why I was surprised two nights ago when she set the receiver in its cradle and buried her head in her hands.

"What's wrong?" I asked warily.

"I just said yes when I should have said no." Mom was staring at the phone like she wished it would disappear.

"Huh?"

"A few days ago, Shira was telling me how the only way to get a job in Manhattan is by knowing someone."

"Because there are so many people, right?"

Mom nodded. "So Shira just called with good news. A friend of a friend is the vice principal of a junior high that's hiring an art teacher, and she can get me an interview."

"That's great!" I exclaimed, so enthusiastically that my voice cracked.

"I don't know." Mom shook her head. "Maybe I should call Shira back. I'm just not up for more rejection right now."

"But how will you know unless you try?" I asked.

"Easier said than done," Mom said as she began filling up a jug for the plants.

I guess she hadn't noticed that I'd already watered them that morning.

Eli has been eating dinner with people from the gardens every Tuesday, so I've only seen him once, in passing. Becca and I were stepping into the lobby, and there he was, head to toe in dirt, mumbling something about having forgotten his heavy-duty gardening gloves. As Becca explained that his responsibilities include digging and weeding, I couldn't stop thinking about the look of surprise on his face when he saw us. Or how blue his eyes appeared when surrounded by the smudges of soil on his cheeks and forehead.

A few minutes later, as Becca and I scooped vanilla ice cream onto chocolate chip cookies, I caught sight of a note thumbtacked to the corkboard next to the phone. I moved closer, pretending to be rinsing my fingers. *E—Jenna called about tomorrow night.* My fires of curiosity were stoked yet again. Who is this Jenna character? Eli's girlfriend? When Becca appeared next to me, I jumped guiltily, though I'm not quite sure why. I mean, should *she* care that I saw the message? And, while we're at it, should *I* care?

The Jenna mystery was finally solved on the first day of the heat wave. Becca and I had taken the crosstown bus home instead of walking across the park as usual. *Mistake #1.* We wound up waiting at the bus stop for twenty sweltering minutes before packing into a vehicle that crept so slowly I wouldn't have been surprised if the driver powered it with his feet, like on *The Flintstones*. By the time we hit the West Side, I was coated with sweat, especially my underarms, which were soaking through to my tank top.

It took a half hour of recuperating in their air-conditioned living room before either of us could muster the energy to fetch lemonade from the refrigerator. But after we'd downed two glasses each, Becca disappeared in search of a deck of cards to play spit.

Kitty and I were obsessed with spit in junior high, so much so that Dad jokingly warned us about carpal tunnel syndrome, like you can get from working long hours at a computer. Spit is this addictive game where you race to get rid of your cards before the other person. It never fails to get me completely wired. One time, I actually bit Kitty's queen of diamonds after I'd lost a round, leaving a full imprint of my teeth across the golden crown.

It's been a while since the spit years, so I was rusty at first, missing obvious plays. But after a few minutes I caught up to speed, walloping Becca in four consecutive rounds. Midway through a heated hand, I was slamming down cards while Becca howled because her ace was stuck to the hardwood floor, when I suddenly got this feeling that we weren't alone. I glanced up, only to see Eli, two other guys and a girl standing in the doorway of the living room, watching us.

"*Spit!*" Becca slapped the smaller pile.

I sat up, tucking strands of hair behind my ears. Eli was to the far left. Next to him was a stocky guy whose sandy hair hung shaggily over his eyes. The other guy, much taller with broad shoulders and orange-tinted sunglasses, had his arm slung around the neck of a girl who I knew, by some kind of instinct, was Jenna.

Jenna was skinny, with boy-short dark hair, wine-colored lipstick and clunky black sandals. She re-minded me of a coyote. I wondered if Phoebe would agree.

"What are you doing home so early?" Becca asked, dealing her hand for the next round. I still hadn't col-lected my cards from the last one.

"They canceled gardening because of the heat," Eli mumbled, fidgeting with his bead-and-hemp neck-lace.

Eli remained in the doorway as the two guys, who introduced themselves as Shay and Alex, flopped onto the couch. Shay grabbed the remote control and switched on MTV. Alex grabbed Jenna, pulling her toward him.

"Wheeeeew!" she shrieked, tumbling onto his lap, knocking off his sunglasses.

"How 'bout it, Rosenthal," Alex hollered as he secured his shades, "aren't you gonna get us some grub?"

Eli started toward the kitchen. Jenna leaped off Alex's lap and chirped, "I'll help!"

As Jenna trotted after him, Alex cracked up. Shay, who'd just explained that heat triggers his asthma, began puffing at his inhaler.

Becca and I resumed playing, but I felt self-conscious with the guys sitting right there on the couch.

"Are you playing spit?" Shay asked.

I nodded.

Becca flung down a succession of nine, ten, jack, queen, jack, even though I had a jack waiting in my hand the whole time.

"You just moved here, right?"

I glanced up at Shay. He blew his bangs off his forehead, but they landed right back where they'd been. How did he know I wasn't from the city? All I'd told him was my first name.

"*Spit!*" Becca cried, slapping the pile with a single card.

Eli and Jenna returned with a six-pack of Coke, a bag of pretzel sticks and the rest of the chocolate chip cookies from last week. Eli plopped the snacks on the coffee table while Jenna made a big production of delivering the Cokes to each person individually. She didn't look me in the eye when she gave me mine. Though a few minutes later, I noticed her checking me out, in that scrutinizing way that girls tend to do to each other. *Up, down, over, back. Pause at the boobs. Pause at the thighs.*

"*Spit! I won!*" Becca screamed after slaughtering me in the next two rounds.

Jenna pumped the volume on the television. *The Real World* was just beginning.

"Do you want to keep playing in my room?" Becca asked me, scooping up her cards.

I don't know what came over me as I said, "No, thanks."

Mistake #2.

As soon as Becca was gone, I regretted it immediately. Surveying the room, I was transported back to 1492, the lone native standing on a beach as the *Nina,* the *Pinta* and the *Santa Maria* docked at the Canary Islands. I grabbed a handful of pretzels.

Meanwhile, Jenna and Alex chattered away as if I weren't even there. A few times, Shay tried to bring me into the conversation, but I didn't really know what to say to them.

I started to worry that I smelled bad. Luckily, the sweat on my tank top had dried already. When no one was looking, I swiped my hand under my armpit and brought it up to my nose. *Not bad. At least I can rule that out.*

"How do I look?" Jenna asked. Some guys on *The Real World* were discussing pot, so she was pinching a pretzel stick between her thumb and pointer finger and sucking in rapidly, as if it was a joint.

"I know something you'd look even better sucking," Alex said, grinning.

"Yeah," Jenna retorted, "except the pretzel would fill up more of my mouth!"

Alex pinned Jenna against a couch cushion and began tickling her. As Jenna squealed, I groaned inwardly. I've seen her type before, the kind of girl whose impertinence to guys results in their lusting after her. Except for Eli. I mean, he'd barely spoken, so I couldn't get a sense of his feelings for her. But she definitely wasn't teasing him. And from the way she kept glancing at him, making references to prior conversations they'd had, it was obvious there was *something* going on.

Two people on *The Real World* were getting in an argument. The guy, a premed student by day and a cross-dresser by night, had apparently borrowed his housemate's fishnet stockings, torn a hole in them and slipped them back in her drawer.

"Remember the last time we watched this, Eli?" Jenna asked. "Didn't they get in a fight then too?"

"I don't remember." Eli shrugged.

"What do you think it takes to get on a show like that?" Shay asked, fiddling with his inhaler.

"You have to have something quirky about you," Alex said, "something cool and unusual."

"I bet you think you'd be perfect for it!" Jenna swatted at his sunglasses.

As Alex dodged Jenna, I glanced over at Eli, just in time to catch him looking at me. He turned away quickly, grabbed a chocolate chip cookie and gobbled it in one bite.

"Of all of us," Shay said, "who would be most likely to get on *The Real World*?"

"You couldn't pay me a million dollars to do it." Jenna swigged her Coke. "No way is someone filming the inside of my bedroom."

"I don't think they allow X-rated content on MTV." Alex chuckled.

"Screw you!" Jenna shrieked.

"Sure." Alex dove at her waist, tickling her again. "Then I could join every other guy in this city!"

As Jenna writhed next to him on the couch, Shay ignored her and asked, "What about Sammie? I think she could do it."

I froze. Eli shoved another cookie in his mouth, this time with the voracity of Cookie Monster.

"I don't think so." Jenna wriggled away from Alex, addressing me directly for the first time. "You're too—"

"Absolutely, completely average," I cut in. *Mistake #3*. I'd meant to finish her sentence before she said something like *pathetic and ugly*, but it wound up sounding stupid.

"If you insist," Jenna said, smacking her burgundy lips together. "I was just going to say 'fresh-faced,' like Eli."

We all glanced over at Eli. He shoved a third cookie in his mouth, even though he couldn't possibly have finished chewing the others. Maybe he was experiencing air deprivation due to the food lodged in his throat, but his face was as red as a fire engine.

CHAPTER FIFTEEN

"If you insist?" Phoebe boomed across the dog run the next morning. "She said, 'If you insist'?"

"Yeah . . . that's pretty much what she said."

We were sitting on the bench that was shaded by an umbrella of leafy trees. With the heat wave still in full blast, the temperature was already in the upper nineties, without the slightest hint of a breeze. But this time Phoebe had brought along a doggie dish and a bottle of water.

"We're obviously dealing with one insecure little bitch! Jenna's obviously threatened by you."

"By me?"

"Isn't it obvious?"

"Why would someone like *her* be threatened by

someone like *me*? And anyway, I'm probably more insecure than all of them, and I'd still never say something like that. . . ."

"First of all"—Phoebe leaned over to refill the dish at our feet as Moxie lapped up the remaining water—"coyotes are so skittish and unpredictable. And second of all, Jenna's *obviously* the more insecure one. Look at the way she had to put you down to make herself feel better."

"You've got a point. . . ."

"I mean, *everyone* is insecure to some degree," Phoebe continued, "but it doesn't mean we can go around dishing out insults whenever we feel like it."

"Are you?"

"Where do I begin?"

"But I just thought . . . you just seem so confident. . . ."

"To quote my sister, Charlotte, 'Confidence and insecurity are not mutually exclusive,' " Phoebe said, folding her arms across her chest. "For instance, deep down, I like myself. But I also wish I weren't such a runt. I wish the guys at school didn't think of me as a buddy type. I wish I could fill more than a jog bra—"

"Are you kidding?" I interrupted. "I wish I could fill up *just* a jog bra!"

"Are *you* kidding? I would kill for yours. . . ."

"You can have them!"

"Okay." Phoebe giggled. "Let's make a dual appointment with a plastic surgeon. Whatever they take from yours they can siphon into mine!"

"Gross"—I made a face—"but you've got yourself a deal."

I glanced at the people strolling down the street, sipping iced coffees. Everyone seemed to be moving more slowly these past few days and it was catching me off guard. I guess I'd grown accustomed to the fast clip of the city.

"Doesn't it feel like a big catch twenty-two?" I asked.

"What do you mean?"

"It seems like guys only go out with girls who've had boyfriends before, like they have this stamp of approval that they're 'girlfriend material.' "

Phoebe nodded. "You can't get it unless you've had it but you must have it in order to get it."

"Something like that . . ."

"That's why my only date so far has been in a chat room with Mountainking."

"Do you think it will always be this way?" I asked.

Phoebe adjusted the Velcro on her knee brace. "Charlotte says it gets better in your twenties. That guys start appreciating women who have something to say."

"But I don't want to wait until then."

"I know." Phoebe scrunched up her nose as she began ripping the Velcro back and forth. After a minute she said, "Remember the other day, when we were talking about birth control pills?"

I nodded. We'd had a long discussion about the Pill when I told her that Kitty had started taking it after Jack got a battery of tests for sexually transmitted diseases, so they wouldn't have to use condoms. We both agreed that when we have a serious relationship that's exactly what we'll do too.

Especially since condoms are so icky, Phoebe had added.

How do you know? I'd asked. A few years ago, I'd stumbled across a pack of lubricated condoms in Dad's desk drawer while I was searching for a hole-punch. I didn't open them or anything. But I did check back a week later, only to discover that two were missing, which made me feel really strange inside.

That's when Phoebe told me how she once swiped a condom from Charlotte's toiletries bag. *You wouldn't believe how big it got,* she grinned, describing how she'd filled it with water from the bathroom faucet. When she got to the part where she flung it out her third-story window and watched it explode on the sidewalk, she was laughing so hard she could barely finish.

But this time around she was solemn.

"I went to my dermatologist yesterday and she wants me to go on the Pill." Phoebe paused. "I haven't even gone to first base yet and I'm starting birth control pills."

"Why?"

"For my skin. They say the Pill can clear up acne."

We were quiet again. This was the first time Phoebe had mentioned her complexion. I wouldn't say it's horrible, mostly rough reddish patches and a few painful-looking pimples, but it's the kind of thing that always looks worse to the person who has it.

I shaded my eyes from the sun. Maybe I should fill her in on Mom and Dad after all. About the lump I got in my throat upon hearing Dad's voice on the answering machine yesterday, something for Mom about health insurance forms. Or how Mom forgot to order an air conditioner until this morning, two days into the most severe heat wave in years. Now they're saying they can't deliver it until the end of the week, which seems pointless because the equatorial temperatures may well be over by then.

I struggled to take a shallow breath.

"Sammie?" Phoebe asked, the hint of a smile on her lips.

"Yeah?"

"Charlotte told me something else too."

"What?"

"She says coyotes are the most common roadkill in the Southwest. That some people even swerve their cars to hit them."

"Really?"

"No one would *ever* swerve toward a chocolate Lab."

"Thanks." I smiled too. "Thanks a lot."

✦　✦　✦

When Phoebe showed up at the dog run on Monday, she had a camera strapped around her neck.

"What's that for?"

We'd arrived at the exact same time, so we were standing on the sidewalk outside the dog run. Moxie was sniffing Phoebe's knee brace. Dogma was sniffing Moxie's hindquarters.

"Mountainking." Phoebe moaned. "When we were chatting online last night, he wrote that he's going on a date with the fry girl at McDonald's, where he works."

"Oh, no." I leaned against the metal gate.

"It gets worse," Phoebe said. "I wrote back that that's fine with me because I've had a boyfriend all along and we're practically engaged."

"Oh, no," I said again.

"Oh, yes. I regretted it the instant I sent it."

"What did he say?"

"Here's the worst part. He wrote, I quote, 'I'll believe that when I see it, as in a photograph of the two of you together.' "

"So what did you say?"

"Here's the *worst* part. I wrote, I quote, 'Could you ask anything easier of me?' " Phoebe leaned forward onto the fence, burying her head in her hands. "Oh, Sammie, what have I gotten myself into?"

"Can't you just scan an image of any couple? I could probably dig up one of Kitty and Jack."

"I would," Phoebe wailed, "except he knows what I look like! I dug through shoe boxes of photos last night, but the only men I have pictures with are my dad and brother. And I can't do the incest thing, not even for Mountainking."

"So where from here?"

Phoebe straightened up again, lifted the camera over her head and handed it to me.

"Congratulations." She grinned. "You have just become a professional photographer."

"But . . ." I glanced up and down Columbus, where the majority of people were executive types hurrying to the subway, and parents pushing drooling babies in strollers. "Who?"

"You just take the pictures," she said, "and leave *that* up to me."

Phoebe grabbed my hand and steered us toward Central Park. The heat wave, which had lingered all week, was finally supposed to break today. The radio was predicting severe thundershowers by early afternoon. But that was pretty hard to believe, seeing that the sky was clear and blue, without a single cloud.

Once we were in the park, Phoebe suggested we head to the Boathouse. That's this place where you can rent rowboats to take onto the small lake, but they also have a fancy restaurant and a snack bar.

"Where the food is," Phoebe sang, "is where the boys are!"

"But how?"

She just pressed her fingers over her lips as she hurried me along. I gripped Moxie's leash with one hand, and with the other I steadied the camera so it wouldn't bounce against my chest.

Phoebe treated us to two iced teas as we settled outside the Boathouse, fastening the dogs to the wooden picnic table. There were a few people milling around, mostly tourists, but Phoebe remained optimistic.

"I'd take a *seeeexy* Italian lover any daaaay," she drawled, attempting some accent that sounded anything but Mediterranean.

As I stirred sugar into my drink, I spotted a guy, probably in his late twenties, carrying a newspaper under his arm.

"What about him?" I whispered, pointing my chin in his direction.

"Too old." Phoebe wrinkled her nose. "He'd look like a pedophile."

After a few minutes, I noticed a lanky guy, much closer to our age, chaining his bike to the wrought-iron fence.

"How about him?"

"Too tall." Phoebe shook her head. "He'd make me look like a midget."

We'd just finished our iced teas when Phoebe sucked in her breath. A family of three, most likely from out of town, was ambling by us. The mother was carrying a Manhattan guidebook. The father was carrying a video camera. The clean-cut teenage son looked like he'd rather be getting a root canal without Novocain.

"Just right," she murmured, heading toward them.

"But Phoebe . . . ," I whispered. I had no idea how she was going to attempt this.

"Follow me," she said, beckoning, "and get ready to snap."

I had to lift my gaping jaw off the pavement as I watched Phoebe explain to the family that we were interns at *Seventeen* and had an assignment to photograph "everyday" teenagers for an upcoming issue. Before I knew it, the parents stepped aside, the father started his camcorder and Phoebe waltzed up to the guy and latched her arm around his waist.

I snapped a picture.

"Maybe you should take another," the mother said, "in case it doesn't come out."

The guy scowled.

Phoebe beamed.

I snapped wildly.

"You definitely have more balls than I do," I told Phoebe as soon as they'd disappeared down the path.

"It's not that hard." Phoebe grinned. "And it's ovaries . . . not balls!"

For the next few hours, as an "intern" at all the major teen magazines, I photographed Phoebe with at least a dozen different guys. Only one turned us down, whispering that he was *running from the Feds.* We weren't sure whether to believe him, but judging from the way his eyes darted suspiciously around, we weren't going to challenge him either. There was only one shot left on the film when gray clouds started to form in the sky.

"Uh-oh." Phoebe glanced upward. "We should head home."

"There's one thing we have to do first," I said, wiping mustard off my fingers with a napkin. Phoebe and I had just split a soft pretzel.

"What are you . . ."

But I didn't stick around to explain. Instead I tossed her the camera and marched up to a guy with reddish brown hair and a goatee.

"Excuse me?" I asked. My hands started shaking, so I stuffed them in my pockets.

"Yeah?"

"We're interns at *Jump* and need to take photos of everyday . . ." I paused.

"Sure." He grinned, slinging his arm around my shoulder. "I'm all yours!"

When he walked away, I couldn't wipe this gigantic smile off my face.

Phoebe dashed up to me and gave me a big hug.

"Who's got the ovaries now?" she asked. "And with an Airedale at that!"

Just then, a drop of rain plopped onto my arm. I untied the dogs as Phoebe sheltered the camera under her shirt, and we started across the park. We'd just reached the spot where Phoebe and I usually say good-bye, when lightning streaked the sky, followed two seconds later by a loud clap of thunder. Dogma froze, huddling close to the ground.

"What should I do?" I shouted. It was pouring by now, rain dripping off my cheeks, my nose, my lips.

"He's petrified of thunder," Phoebe shouted back, both of her hands still on the camera. "He's not going anywhere."

"I can carry him to your place if you want."

"But it's ten blocks up."

"That's okay."

I scooped up a cowering Dogma and carried him to the door of Phoebe's building, a brownstone I'd never seen before. I hadn't even known what block she lived on. As Phoebe started up the stairs, she dragged her braced leg behind her. She had invited me in, but since the news had said the storm would continue into the evening, I thought it best to hurry back to our apartment, especially since Moxie was with me.

I ran the rest of the way home, stopping only twice to catch my breath. By the time I reached our building, it was so dark out that it looked like evening, except for the occasional flash of lightning illuminating the sky.

As we waited for the elevator, Moxie shook, spraying water all over the mirror in the lobby. I glanced at my reflection. *Ugh.* I looked like I'd just plunged into a lake fully clothed. My hair was plastered to my head and my white T-shirt, clinging to my skin, revealed the complete outline of my bra.

"Hey there."

The elevator doors had just opened. J.D. was standing inside. Holding an umbrella. Grinning.

"Got caught in the rain?"

He kept grinning. He stepped around me. He couldn't peel his eyes away from my boobs. If Moxie hadn't dragged me into the elevator, I doubt I would have moved.

"Sara, right?"

Sara? Didn't Mom tell him my name the first time we met?

"Sammie," I said through chattering teeth.

"Right." J.D. nodded. "Sammie."

As the doors closed, Moxie shook muddy droplets all over my knocking knees.

The phone was ringing as I unlocked our door. Racing to get it, I bumped into the air conditioner in the entranceway, exactly where the delivery guy had left it three days ago. I caught the phone on the fourth ring, just as the answering machine picked up.

"Hello?" I pressed the Stop button. It made five loud beeps as the tape began to rewind.

"I found out who it is." Kitty's voice was barely audible.

"What?" I asked loudly. Moxie was shaking again, right next to the futon this time.

"It's not Jack's ex."

"Who is it?"

"The girl who lives in your house!"

Oscar Mayer Wienerette? I was incredulous. "How do you know?"

It took Kitty ten minutes, between whimpers and wails, to describe how she'd been overcome with a psychic impulse to drive around my cul-de-sac yesterday evening. And what should she spot but Jack's Jeep parked in front of my place? As soon as she'd gotten home, she'd dialed his cell phone. He said he'd call back later, neglecting to mention that *later* wouldn't be till the following morning. And when Kitty confronted him about it, he neither denied nor apologized, just saying that his head was *all messed up right now.*

As Kitty sobbed, I began to shiver. Partially because that's a horrendous thing for your first lover to tell you. And partially because of the irony that the girl who inhabits *my* room is probably fooling around with Kitty's boyfriend. But mostly, I was overcome by the notion that Kitty, for all her perfection, had been jettisoned for the new kid on the block.

"I feel so awful," Kitty said after a long pause. "Everything in Ithaca reminds me of Jack."

A clap of thunder boomed and Moxie scurried under Mom's bed.

"Sammie?"

"Yeah?"

"Do you think I could come visit you this weekend? I really need to spend time with someone who will listen to me."

Ninety bucks an hour, I was tempted to say, *is my going rate now.* But when I opened my mouth what slipped out instead was: "Yeah, sure you can."

"Great," Kitty sniffled, "because I already called Greyhound about bus fares for Friday."

When we hung up, I continued to shake. I really needed to take a hot shower. As I peeled off my T-shirt, I remembered what Mom had said the other day: *I just said yes when I should have said no.*

Oh, well. I sighed, flinging my bra and underwear into a heap on the floor. *What's done is done.*

CHAPTER SIXTEEN

Mom didn't cancel her interview with the friend of
Shira's friend after all. At first I took it as a good
sign. On Thursday evening, she pulled *Feel the Fear
and Do It Anyway* off the bookshelf. As I was hunched
over the subway map, figuring out the best route to the
bus station, she kept murmuring and reading me pas-
sages from chapter 9, "Just Nod Your Head—Say
'Yes!'"

So I'm not sure what happened between then and
Friday morning, when her interview was scheduled at the
private school. I awoke to the sound of Mom grinding coffee beans in the kitchen. As I padded into the bathroom, I
noticed her tan summer suit laid out across the bed.

But when I actually got a look at her, sitting at the

kitchen table swirling her coffee around in its mug, I knew something was up. Her face was pale, the half-moons under her eyes practically black.

"I didn't get a wink of sleep last night," she said glumly.

I poured myself a glass of grapefruit juice, two for the price of one at the local supermarket. As I sliced a bialy and dropped it in the toaster, I noticed Mom's pen-and-ink cityscape crumpled in the kitchen trash. I felt my throat tighten.

"I'm not even sure I even want to be an art teacher anymore. . . ." Mom's voice trailed off.

When the bialy popped up, Mom jolted forward, like she'd gotten an electric shock. Just as she did, her blouse, slippery in its dry cleaning bag, slid off the bed, the metal hanger clattering against the floor.

"You look stressed," Phoebe pronounced a half hour later. "I can see it in your face."

We were sitting on a bench in the dog run, watching Moxie and Dogma romp around with a pair of pugs.

"I don't know." I sighed. "There's a lot going on."

"Kitty?"

I nodded. "That's part of it."

"Just so you know, my offer still stands."

Yesterday, when I'd told Phoebe that I wasn't exactly thrilled about Kitty's visit, she'd suggested I bring her up to the dog run.

I'll cat-sit. Phoebe had giggled. *Get it? Like her name is Kitty?*

I got it, I'd groaned.

But I really hope it doesn't come to that. The thought of introducing them makes me feel uneasy, especially since Kitty has this tendency to be ultrapossessive of me. Like this past spring when she got all huffy because I'd hitched a ride home with a girl from chorus rather than lingering until her softball practice ended.

Just as we were saying good-bye, Phoebe fished around in her backpack and produced a rubbery potato-shaped object.

"Here." She handed it to me. "You can have this."

"What is it?" I asked, gripping the tightly packed beanbag.

"It's a stress ball. Squeezing it is supposed to help reduce tension."

I massaged it in my hand. I can definitely see how this could absorb negative energy. But why do I have a feeling that there aren't enough stress balls in the universe to reduce the amount of anxiety inside me?

✦　✦　✦

I arrived at Port Authority twenty minutes before Kitty's bus was due. Pacing at the gate, I squeezed the stress ball. The bus terminal reeked of a nauseating blend of gasoline and body odor. If Phoebe thought my face looked tense before, she should see me now, after I'd just listened to the message back at our apartment.

Mom wasn't home when I dropped off Moxie. I'd assumed she was at her interview already, until I noticed the red light flashing on the answering machine. I'd pressed the play button, only to hear:

Beep

Nine-forty-seven A.M.

Hello. (A woman paused to clear her throat.) *This is Karen Drabick, Shira Rosenthal's friend. I'm sorry to hear that the interview isn't taking place after all. Please get in touch with me if you'd like to reschedule. Thanks so much.*

Beep. Beep. Beep. Beep. Beep.

Kitty was the first one off the bus. She was wearing khaki shorts and a tank top, with a trendy messenger bag strapped across her chest. I saw her at least a minute before she saw me. As I watched her glancing around the terminal, I felt like I was seeing her for the first time—this tall, Nordic, confident-looking stranger. It made me want to turn and bolt in the other direction.

"There you are." Kitty strode toward me. Her eyes looked tired but her face was tan, her nose sprinkled with the freckles that crop up every summer. "I didn't see you at first."

As we hugged, I was swamped with emotion. This is

Kitty Lundquist. My soul sister for eight years. One of my only links to my life in Ithaca. Maybe I've been overreacting. Maybe all this business with Mom and Dad has screwed with my head. Maybe it'll be good to spend the weekend with her after all.

Less than an hour later, here's why I would eat those thoughts:

1. We hadn't gone two stops on the subway when Kitty mentioned Marla Mueller for the twenty-third time. I guess I was distracted, trying to determine whether we should board the uptown local or express train, because I didn't register who Marla Mueller was. When I finally asked Kitty, she snapped: *Marla Mueller is* only *the person who lives in your house, who's screwing* my *boyfriend. Haven't you been paying attention?*

2. When we arrived back at the apartment, Mom was buried under her covers with the shades drawn. As I closed the door so we wouldn't disturb her, I whispered to Kitty: *Now you see what I'm talking about.* To which she replied: *Actually, I don't think your place is as small as you described.*

3. I finally decided that the only way I'd survive this would be to bring Kitty to Central Park, to the dog run, anything but stewing in the apartment. And

that's when it started to rain, for the first time since last week. And rain. And rain.

✦ ✦ ✦

By Saturday evening, I was about to go out of my mind. The rain was still coming down, mostly just drizzle by this point. Kitty and I had only braved it once, when we dashed out to Tower Records to rent a movie. We hadn't been able to agree on anything. Kitty wanted to rent a comedy, *to bring her up*. I suggested tear-jerking dramas, *to show that our trials aren't as arduous as we think*. Slapstick won out, with Kitty insisting on the new Austin Powers movie.

I handed my video card to the guy behind the counter. He was pale and slight, with metallic silver fingernails and lusterless black hair that had *home dye job* written all over it.

"Austin Powers." He nodded at me in a subdued, goth sort of way. "Cool choice."

"Thanks," I said. "I actually—"

But Kitty cut me off. "She wanted a Julia Roberts movie. I had to twist her arm to get this."

He raised his pierced-with-several-hoops eyebrow as his gaze panned from me to Kitty and rested there. "Julia Roberts is *so* cheesy."

"Amen," Kitty answered, flashing her I-know-you-find-me-sexy-but-I'm-way-way-out-of-your-league smile.

Once Kitty and I were on the street, I pulled Phoebe's stress ball out of my pocket and began working it in my fist.

Shira was there when we returned to the apartment. Yesterday evening, when Mom finally dragged herself out of bed, she'd called Shira to explain how she'd gotten last-minute cold feet about the interview. Shira must have reassured her that she'd do it when she was ready because Mom had sighed and said, *At this point it feels like I'll never be ready,* which made me doubly relieved that Kitty was still in the shower. Before they'd hung up, I heard them make a plan to check out a new Thai place tonight.

As I was setting my umbrella in the tub to dry, Kitty explained to Shira that her real name is Katarina and her father is originally from Stockholm.

"So that's where you get your height," Shira said.

"Actually, my maternal grandmother is over six feet."

I flopped onto the futon, watching Kitty dazzle Shira with her grace and eloquence. Adults are always impressed upon meeting Kitty, shaking their head when they discover she's still in high school.

Shira set her empty coffee cup in the sink as Mom searched the closet for a light sweater.

"That's quite a necklace." Kitty pointed to the ropes of turquoise and silver around Shira's neck.

"Thanks." Shira reached up and touched it. "It's Native American, from the Southwest."

"Was it made by the Navajo?"

"Yes." Shira nodded enthusiastically. "Someone I work with took a trip to New Mexico."

The second they were out the door, Kitty flounced down next to me. "Your mom has always gravitated toward Earth women."

"What are you talking about?" I asked.

"Shira's the original Venus of Willendorf." Kitty crammed a pillow under her tank top to emphasize the curvaceously chunky prehistoric statuette that we'd learned about during the art and culture unit of global studies last year. "And what was up with her never-ending necklace? She looked like some kind of rapper."

"Why did you tell her you liked it?"

"I didn't say I liked it. I said it was *quite* a necklace. Which, I might add, it was."

"You still shouldn't have said anything."

Kitty turned to me. "What's eating you? Ever since we left the video store you've been acting like someone died."

"Nothing," I said as I stomped into the kitchen and started up water for hot chocolate. How could I tell Kitty that I was sick of hearing her drone on about her life? Whether Marla Mueller would give Jack the *you-know-what* that Kitty had been denying him. Whether Marla Mueller was a mid–high-school crisis or the Real Thing. Whether she'd put on a few pounds over the summer. And if so, whether she should go on this new protein diet her father has been recommending to his patients.

As Kitty yanked at her nonexistent love handles, I was tempted to say, *Unless there's body fat in freckles, shut your fucking trap!* If there's anything that can push me over the edge, it's girls who are bonier than runway models complaining that the skin on their thighs is cellulite.

Right before we went to sleep, Kitty suggested we give ourselves pedicures with the polish she'd brought. I'd selected Brazenberry, which I splashed on in about a minute and a half. Kitty, after inserting a cotton ball between each toe, meticulously applied two coats of Teak Rose. As she waited for the second layer to dry, she glanced up at me.

"We really are different, aren't we?"

I didn't say anything right away. But later, as we were tucked under the sheets on the futon, I was ready to talk more about it. I was lying on my back, with my hands under my head, my elbows splaying out like wings. Kitty was turned on her side, with her foot touching my shin.

"Kitty?"

"Mmm . . ."

"About what you said before, about us being different . . ."

"Mmmhmmm . . ."

I paused, trying to find the right words to express how it seems like we've grown apart this summer. And how it's really important that she listens to me also. I wanted to say it in a diplomatic way, so it didn't make her defensive but still got the point across.

That's when I noticed Kitty's steady, rhythmic breathing. I sat up and leaned across her. Even though the lights were out, I could tell she was fast asleep.

I settled back down again, shifting positions so she was no longer touching my leg. Maybe it's not so much that we've grown apart as that I've grown up. That I've been dealing with a pretty tough situation, not high-school drama but a real-life crisis. That I'm not the same person I was two months ago.

It's strange. I always thought Kitty and I would be best friends forever, e-mailing daily throughout college, raising our kids in adjoining backyards, barbecuing skewers of shish kebab on warm summer evenings.

Then again, I always thought my parents would be *RozandJames* forever, and look where *that* got me. Who knows? I mean, it's only a trial separation so far. But sometimes it seems like a separation just prolongs the inevitable, the Big D. Like with this much water under the bridge, how can we ever go back to the way things used to be, all of us living together in the Ithaca house? And let's say we do, how can I be sure it won't fall apart again?

But if there's anything I've learned in the past few months, it's that the only thing that's certain in life is that nothing in life is certain.

✦ ✦ ✦

The rain finally stopped on Sunday morning. When Kitty popped up a little after seven, the sky was clear and the sun was beaming through the windows.

"I don't think Marla Mueller is going to last, you-know-whats and all," she said, inspecting her toenails.

I yawned loudly. I swear, if I hear the name Marla Mueller once more, I'm going to slap duct tape across Kitty's mouth.

"There's someone I want you to meet," I said, stretching my arms above my head.

I was at the end of my rope. Kitty's bus was at one-fifteen, which left us six more hours. Which meant that if Kitty mentioned Marla Mueller every five minutes, a conservative estimate, I could potentially hear her name seventy-two more times. Which, in the end, would require a lot of duct tape.

"Didn't you hear me?" Kitty asked. "I said, I don't think Marl—"

"Well, I said, there's someone I want you to meet."

Kitty glared at me. "A guy?"

Why does Kitty look so shocked by the notion that I would introduce her to a guy, as if she's the only one who can commune with the opposite sex?

"No." I glared back. "Just a friend."

"As long as I can get some coffee on the way. I don't think I've ever gone this long without a cup of coffee."

We'd only been in the dog run a few minutes when Phoebe arrived. But it was long enough for Kitty to complain that:

1. it stank of dog-doo.
2. wood chips were scuffing her new sandals.
3. the sight of slobbery slaver dangling from the snout of a nearby mutt was enough to make her want to puke up her iced cappuccino.

I was about to ask her where she came up with *slaver* when Phoebe unlatched the metal gate and jogged toward us.

"You must be Kitty!"

Kitty seemed surprised that Phoebe knew her name.

"I'm Phoebe . . . and this is Dogma."

As Dogma wagged his stubby tail, Kitty looked Phoebe up and down, pausing at her knee brace. Phoebe flopped down next to me on the bench so I was sitting in the middle. I massaged the stress ball in my hand. I could already feel tension in the air.

"Funny," Phoebe said, after a bit, "I didn't picture you as a collie."

Kitty made a face. "*What* are you talking about?"

"I have this theory," Phoebe said, "that every person looks like a dog."

"A *dog*?"

"It's an interesting thing to figure out"—I shifted positions so I blocked Kitty's view of Phoebe—"like I'm a chocolate Lab and Phoebe's a Jack Russell terrier."

"*A chocolate Lab and a Jack Russell terrier?*" Kitty curled her lip disdainfully, as if she were the Queen of England and Phoebe and I were flea-ridden peasants begging for a hunk of moldy bread. "I'm sorry, but I'm not about to go around telling people I look like a dog. No thank you."

We were all quiet for a few minutes, but not good quiet. More the kind of quiet where you can feel tension mounting. After a while, as Phoebe began tossing a stick to the dogs, Kitty started up again about Marla Mueller. But only to me, as if Phoebe weren't two feet away.

Before I knew it, Phoebe leaned forward, fiddling with the Velcro on her knee brace. "If you ask me," she said, "cheating on someone when you're in a monogamous relationship is like holding a loaded gun to their head."

Kitty shot an if-looks-could-kill look at Phoebe. I felt the color draining from my face. There are some moments in life when you wish you had one of those "get out of jail free" cards from Monopoly and you could make the entire situation instantaneously disappear.

"I didn't ask you." Kitty's voice was razor sharp. "But while we're at it, how do you know about what happened with my boyfriend?"

"I'm sorry." Phoebe nervously ripped the Velcro back and forth. "I thought it was . . ."

"What *else* did Sammie tell you?"

Turning to Phoebe, I was about to reassure her that she didn't have to say another word, when her face began to crumple.

"Kitty—" I started.

"Did she tell you how her father ditched her and

took off for California? Or that her mother is a self-help-reading basket case? Or—"

Phoebe grabbed her backpack and stood up. "It's time for me to go," she said, not looking either of us in the eye.

I'm sorry, Phoebe. I wanted to get up and run after her. But it was like one of those nightmares where you try to scream and no sound comes out, you try to run and your feet won't move. As I watched Phoebe walk out, her shoulders slumped, a stiff-eared Dogma in tow, I felt like the most awful person on the planet.

"What the *hell* was up with her?" Kitty said as Phoebe turned up Columbus. "Calling me a collie and talking about my boyfriend as if she's some kind of sex-ed instructor? And did you see the way she sprinted in here? I don't think there's anything wrong with that knee of hers."

I couldn't speak. I couldn't think. All I could do was feel furious, so furious that if my fist hadn't been clamped around the stress ball, I probably would have hurled it at Kitty.

"What a freak," Kitty murmured, shaking her head.

"Don't call Phoebe a freak," I said through clenched teeth.

Kitty shot me a cold glance. "I hardly think you're

one to be making judgment calls, after you go and spill my personal life to the entire world."

"I told one person. *My friend.* And what do you think you just did, telling Phoebe about my parents?"

"If she's such a great friend, then why hadn't you told her yourself?"

I swallowed several times. I could feel anger building up in my throat.

Kitty didn't wait for a response. "You've changed, Sammie," she said, her pale eyes narrowing. "I've been feeling it all weekend. You've changed . . . and I have to say, I don't like it."

"You don't like it because I'm not your personal therapist anymore."

"You know what?" Kitty stood up so quickly her plastic cup toppled onto the ground. "You're a freak just like her. You two freaks should be awfully happy together!"

"Well, at least I'm not an egomaniac!" I shouted back, so loudly that some people paused outside the metal gate.

And that's when Kitty marched out of the dog run, her head tilted in the air, as if she were some kind of celebrity. I must have been digging my fingernails into the stress ball, because the next thing I knew it exploded in my hand, millions of sand grains filtering onto the wood chips at my feet.

CHAPTER SEVENTEEN

I once heard this saying, "The best thing about hitting your head against a brick wall is how good it feels when you stop." That sums up how I feel about Kitty right now. I didn't see her again after our fight because by the time I made it home she'd already flagged a cab to Port Authority. Although I was surprised when Mom recapped Kitty's brief entrance and exit, saying how she'd cited "irreconcilable differences," I also felt a weight lifted off my shoulders, knowing I didn't have to deal with her anymore.

What I'm really worried about is Phoebe. I went to the dog run the following morning, ready with an apology I'd prepared in my head the night before. Even though I know I'm not responsible for Kitty's outburst,

I still feel like I could have prevented it, by following my initial instinct not to introduce them. And I definitely owed Phoebe an explanation about my parents, especially since she's always been so open about everything in her life.

But I was completely unprepared for what awaited me on Monday morning. Nothing. No Phoebe, no Dogma, nothing. I sat on our favorite bench for over an hour, watching waves of dogs and owners come and go. After a while, I started to feel nauseous, probably from the thick odor of dog crap, which I'd never noticed until Kitty had pointed it out.

I must have looked pretty distressed when I got home because Mom launched into a sermon about how *friendships have their ebbs and flows. How you and Kitty have a long history together, and with some breathing room, a long future, too.*

Is that what you and Dad are doing? I wanted to say. *Ebbing and flowing? Well, please let me know when you've stopped being a tidal pool and started being parents again.*

But I didn't. I was too busy flipping through the phone book for the number of the veterinarian Phoebe once mentioned she takes Dogma to. The patch on Moxie's back had improved for a while, after I'd washed her with that shampoo Charlotte had recommended. But in the past few days it has returned, and much worse this time. It's raw and pink and she won't stop gnawing at it, even though I'm constantly pushing her snout away.

The receptionist at the vet's office was beside himself when I said I knew Phoebe Frank.

"Any friend of Phoebe's is a friend of ours," he chirped.

I felt like bawling on the spot.

But when I tried to schedule something, he informed me that there were no available appointments for several weeks. "We're only open a few days a week in August, since most of our patients are out of town."

"Can you refer me to another vet?"

He paused. I could hear the tap-tapping of a keyboard in the background. "Hold on! We have a cancellation tomorrow at four P.M., if you can swing by then."

I dashed into the other room and made sure Mom could take Moxie over there, since I had to pick up Becca from gymnastics at the same time. Just before we hung up, after I'd spelled Amoxicillin twice, the receptionist said, "Any friend of Dogma's is a friend of ours."

Phoebe would have been thrilled to discover we were going to her vet. She probably would have cracked some joke like *Moxie is as sick as a dog.* Or she would have asked Moxie how she was feeling, waving a stick just out of her reach until she barked, *Rough, rough, rough.*

But Phoebe wasn't in the dog run Tuesday morning either, and I waited for almost two hours this time, hoping to catch her if she decided to come later instead. I wasn't sure what else to do. I mean, we don't even have each other's phone numbers. I know where she lives but I'm not about to march up there, only to find out that she never wants to see my face again.

After lunch on Tuesday, my mood started to spiral downward. I grabbed my guitar, stuck a Post-it to the bathroom mirror reminding Mom about Moxie's appointment, and headed into Central Park. By midafternoon, I was sitting in the Sheep Meadow, which is this gigantic lawn where people lounge around in their bathing suits as if it's a beach, just without the water. I rested my arms on my guitar and looked out at the Midtown skyscrapers looming in the distance. And that's when I noticed the giant digital clock on the side of one of the buildings. And that's when my heart started racing. I was supposed to meet Becca in less than twenty minutes!

Throwing my guitar into its case, I sprinted across the grass and rooted through my pockets for change. Hopefully I could hop on the next crosstown bus, transfer on the East Side and still arrive on time, give or take five minutes.

✦ ✦ ✦

"Whose guitar is this?" I overheard Eli asking Becca.

I paused in the hallway, where I was coming out of the bathroom.

"Sammie's," Becca said.

"She plays guitar?"

I didn't hear Becca respond, but I could picture her sitting on a tall stool, swinging her bare feet. We'd been home for a few minutes, enough time to devour the left-over blueberry pie that had been in the fridge. *Eli hasn't gone to the gardens for two days now,* Becca had explained, *due to a raging case of poison ivy.* He hadn't shown his face since we'd gotten home, but I'd been keeping an eye on the door to his room, which happens to be connected to the kitchen because it was the maid's room in the original apartment.

I headed through the doorway.

"Hey," I said. I was glad I'd picked the blueberry seeds out of my teeth when I'd been in the bathroom.

"Hey." Eli scratched his neck.

His poison ivy wasn't as bad as Becca had described, just some bumpy patches on his cheeks and arms.

"You play guitar?"

I nodded, leaning against the counter.

"What kind of music?"

"Pretty much anything . . . but I really like folk music, old stuff . . ."

Eli's eyes widened. "You like folk music?"

"Oh, no," Becca moaned. Her braces were dotted with blueberry skins. "You've only mentioned Eli's second-favorite obsession, after tree-hugging."

"Yeah," I said, "that's mostly what I play."

"Would you mind playing something?"

I tapped my Birkenstock nervously against the floor, like I was keeping time. I never thought twice about playing in front of Mom, Dad, Kitty or all of Central Park for that matter, but I haven't ever *performed* for someone before.

"Only if you want to," Eli added.

My heart was thumping as I unclasped my case and lifted out my guitar. I sat on a stool, the familiar curves of my instrument pressing against my thighs. I quickly tuned my strings, which tend to slip in warm weather, and began playing Bob Dylan's "Blowin' in the Wind." It was one of the first songs Dad taught me. *A folk singer's staple,* he'd said. I didn't sing or anything, but I've figured out a way to fingerpick the melody so it doesn't just sound like a jumble of chords.

"Wow!" Becca said as soon as I'd finished. "You're really good!"

"Thanks."

I looked over at Eli.

"That was beautiful." Eli caught my eye. "I actually have an early recording of Dylan playing that song."

"Really?" I asked.

"Oh, no," Becca moaned again, "now you're going to hear about his famous record collection!"

"You have a record player?"

"Yeah . . . it used to belong to my dad."

I glanced from Eli to Becca. Neither of them has ever mentioned their father before. But I once noticed this photograph in the living room of a man sitting on a swing, holding a redheaded baby in his lap. Hanging upside down off a neighboring bar was a miniature Eli, maybe five or six years old. They all are smiling, even Becca. When I saw the picture it made me feel sad, because none of them knew that in less than a year, he would be dead.

"Do you want to hear the song?"

"Sure."

Becca patted her hand over her mouth in an exaggerated yawn as she switched on the computer, which is set up in an alcove near the kitchen. "I'm going to do something a little more twenty-first-century."

Eli's tiny room was draped floor to ceiling in brightly colored tapestries and a huge poster of the planet Earth with lettering below it that said Love Your Mother. As I sat cross-legged next to his bed, just a single futon mattress directly on the floor, I watched him dig through a pile of records stacked in an orange milk crate.

"Here it is." Eli held up a battered album with a picture on the cover of a young Bob Dylan walking arm in arm along a snowy street with a long-haired girl.

There was a scratchy sound as the needle dropped onto the record. As Dylan's familiar strumming piped through the speakers, Eli slid over so he was sitting next to me. We didn't say anything throughout the whole song, or the next. But midway through "Masters of War," Eli reached over me to retrieve a tube of Caladryl that was on the crate next to his bed. When he did, his hand brushed against my arm.

He'd just finished smearing the lotion on his neck when he turned to me.

"Sammie?"

"Yeah?"

"I know my mom sort of pushed it on you a while ago—" Eli was screwing and unscrewing the Caladryl cap—"but I'm going camping at Bear Mountain this weekend . . . and the invitation still stands. . . ."

"When are you leaving?" I asked, stalling for time.

"Saturday morning . . . and we get back Sunday afternoon."

My mind suddenly flashed to Jenna. What if she's coming too? I'd rather spend a weekend chained in a torture chamber than with that coyote, but it's not as if I can ask Eli something like that. I began picking at my toenail polish.

"You don't have to tell me right away," Eli added, "you can even decide at the last minute."

"Thanks."

"Just so you know, I didn't invite Jenna. It'll just be me, Shay, my cousin Max and his girlfriend, Ellen."

Eli reached across me again, to put the lotion back on his bedside table. This time, when his hand touched my arm, it rested there for a second, which sent a feeling through my body that made me want to laugh and cry at the same time.

CHAPTER
EIGHTEEN

When I unlocked our front door a half hour later, Moxie galloped out to greet me. I noticed that the raw patch on her back had some bloody crevices where she'd been gnawing it this morning.

"Mom?"

"Ummhmm," Mom called from the bathroom, where she was brushing her teeth.

"What did the vet say?"

I heard the faucet running. After a minute, Mom appeared in the doorway, a dollop of froth in the corner of her mouth. She just stood there for a few seconds with this uncomfortable look on her face.

"What did the vet say?" I repeated, clenching my teeth.

"Sammie . . ."

"You didn't forget, did you?" I suddenly felt all the emotion from the past few days, from Kitty, from Phoebe, from everything, welling up in my throat.

Mom nodded solemnly as she pointed to where *Ten Days to Self-Esteem* was sprawled facedown on her bed. "I was reading . . . somehow the hours just slipped away. I called them a few minutes ago and they're closed for the day."

"How could you? I left you that Post-it and everything!"

"These things happen. . . ."

"These things don't just *happen*. I asked you to do one small thing"—my tone grew louder as I snatched up Mom's book and flung it against the wall—"and you were too consumed with your emotional suffering to care for a poor dog in pain!"

Mom's face paled as she stared at the mark on the wall where her book had made contact. "I think you're overreacting . . . you're being completely unfair. . . ."

"Unfair?" I asked, my voice cracking. "Do you want to talk about unfair?" I stormed around the apartment, the words springing off my tongue faster than I could think. I paused in front of the air conditioner, still in its box in the hallway, exactly where it had been since it was delivered two weeks ago. "Let's talk about how nothing ever gets done around here unless I do it! Let's talk about how I have to worry night and day about our lives!"

Mom froze in the doorway, watching my tirade.

"I know separating with Dad is hard for you," I shouted. "And I know starting over in this city is hard. But it's hard for me too. Dad leaving was the most painful thing . . ."

I paused. I'd never said it out loud before and it was making my throat tighten up.

And that's when Mom slipped into her sandals, not even pulling the straps over her heels, and grabbed her set of keys. As she started out of the apartment, I shouted after her, "Did you ever stop to think how any of this makes me feel?"

But she didn't answer. She just ran out, the toothpaste still on her face, leaving the door swinging on its hinges. As soon as I heard the elevator arrive, I slammed the door as hard as I could. And then, just because I felt like it, I opened the door and slammed it again.

Pacing around the apartment, my hair flipping wildly in front of my eyes, I didn't feel the least bit of remorse. In fact, when I noticed my dictionary sitting on the floor, I slid Dad's card out of the back, quickly scanned the note and dialed his phone number.

I hadn't expected to get his answering machine, but I was so fired up by this point that nothing was going to stop me. When I heard Dad's voice say, *Leave a message after the beep,* I spewed every thought that crossed my mind. All about how life is anything but fine, how Mom had fallen apart, and how, most of all, he had betrayed my belief that he was the one person I could always count on. I was in the middle of a lecture about washing hands of family responsibilities when his machine cut me off. Even though I'd said practically everything, I pressed Redial, listened to his message again and then shouted into the phone, "And by the way, *I'll* tell you when I'm done talking, *not* your stupid machine!"

After I slammed down the phone, I looked out the window for a while, feeling small and alone, yet strangely connected at the same time. I began humming this old Janis Joplin song, "Me and Bobby McGee." There's this part where she sings, *Freedom's just another word for nothing left to lose. . . .*

And that's when it hit me. Over the past few months, I've given up my entire life, my parents have orbited into a galaxy far, far away, my best friend has been completely self-absorbed and now my new friend wants nothing to do with me. But in this inexplicable way, it all makes me free. Free to take risks I wouldn't ordinarily take because, in the end, I haven't got much to lose.

And that's when I realized I had one phone call left to make.

"Hello?" Eli answered on the second ring.

"Hey . . . it's Sammie."

"Hi! Did you just get home?"

"Yeah . . . a few minutes ago."

We were quiet for a second. I gripped the phone tightly in my hand. *Okay, Sammie, now or never.*

"Eli?"

"Yeah?"

"I was thinking . . . about the Bear Mountain trip . . ."

"Yeah?"

"I'd like to come."

"You'd like to come?"

"Yes."

Eli launched into a description of trails and swimming holes, adding how they've got an extra sleeping bag and there will definitely be space for three in the tent. It must have been five minutes before he finally came up for air.

"Sammie?" he asked, right before we hung up.

"Yeah?"

"I'm glad you're coming."

"Me too."

After I got off the phone, I suddenly felt tired, more tired than I've ever felt in my life. I stumbled toward Mom's bed. My arms, my legs, even my eyelids seemed like they were full of cement.

The next thing I knew, Mom was pulling off my sandals and sliding my legs under the sheets.

"No," I mumbled, "I'll move to the futon."

"It's only seven-thirty," Mom whispered, switching off the small lamp next to the bed, "you can stay right here."

I opened my eyes. The room was pretty dark, but then I realized that the shades were drawn. Right before I closed my eyes again, Mom leaned over and kissed me on the forehead. For the first time in months, I didn't try to stop her.

CHAPTER NINETEEN

They always say there's a calm before the storm. In my case, the calm came after. The days following my outburst were uneventful, almost serene. Neither Mom nor I said another word about it, but in a way the air had been cleared. After months of tiptoeing around each other as if we were in a minefield, it was a relief to have finally set off the explosion.

And life after the bomb produced such surprises as:

1. Mom talking her way into an early-morning appointment at the vet's, where they gave Moxie a cortisone shot that reduced her irritation by sundown.

2. The super appearing in our apartment with a measuring tape, promising Mom he'd return soon to install the air conditioner.

3. Friday afternoon, when Uncle Steve called.

I'd been sitting on the futon leafing through *Chicken Soup for the Woman's Soul,* which Mom had picked up at the bookstore a few weeks ago. It actually wasn't so horrible, especially this Maya Angelou poem in the beginning called "Phenomenal Woman." There's this one part where she writes: *It's the reach of my hips . . . the stride of my step.* And then she goes on to describe the things that make her a real woman.

For some reason, it reminds me of Mom. The way she's comfortable in her body, curves and big breasts and all. I wonder if I'll be like that someday too. I hope so.

Mom was nodding and ummhmming. What I gathered from her half of the conversation was that Uncle Steve was inviting us out to Long Island for Labor Day, to swim in their pool. I began flapping the book in the air, trying to let her know that there was no way I would spend the weekend with the Original Asshole. And that's when Mom said something about how we'd love to, but unfortunately we had other plans.

"What other plans?" I asked as soon as she hung up.

"I don't know." Mom shrugged. "I just made it up."

"What about your Lincolnian code of ethics?"

Mom laughed. "Even Abe would blur the truth if he met Uncle Steve."

She crossed the room and sat next to me on the futon.

"I was thinking," she said, "maybe we could drive up to Ithaca over Labor Day weekend. I'd like to pick up my oil paints from the house . . . and if you want we can bring back your bike."

"Mariposa?"

"As long as you promise to only ride it in the park."

I was so shocked that I dropped *Chicken Soup* on the floor. I couldn't believe Mom had changed her mind about Mariposa.

Mom must have sensed my surprise because she quickly added, "I take that as a yes."

I nodded, my mind racing ahead to whether or not I'd let Kitty know I was in Ithaca.

What has surprised me more than anything, though, is the fact that Dad still hasn't called, not since I left that message on his machine. It's not like I expected him to collapse at my feet, begging for forgiveness, but at the very least, I'd imagined a phone call, just to make sure things are okay.

Not that I even have an answer to that. Because they

are and they aren't. For instance, in the past few days, I haven't been having a difficult time breathing. And my throat hasn't been tightening every seven seconds, even when I think about how Phoebe hasn't shown up at the dog run all week.

As I got into bed on Friday night, I wished I had a fairy godmother who could sagely advise me about Phoebe. Suddenly I remembered this time when Phoebe and I were talking about religion.

Have you ever noticed that God spelled backward is dog? she'd asked me, grinning mischievously.

I pressed my face into my pillow. I miss her so much it hurts.

Please, Fairy Dogmother, tell me how to make things better with Phoebe. Because at this point, whatever needs to be done, I'll do it.

✦　✦　✦

I woke up at seven-fifteen on Saturday morning, an hour before my alarm was supposed to go off. I wasn't due at Eli's until ten, so I pulled the sheet over my head and attempted to drift back to sleep. But after lying there for ten minutes with enough adrenaline to run a marathon, I hopped up and tiptoed into the bathroom.

I stood under the shower for a long time, letting the hot spray massage my neck. As much as I'm excited about going to Bear Mountain, I'm also pretty nervous. Like when I remind myself that I barely know Eli or Shay and have never even met Max and Ellen. Or when I remember how Eli said there would be "space for three" in the tent. Which obviously translates to Max and Ellen sharing one tent and Eli, Shay and me sharing the other. Which makes my stomach flip over, seeing that I've never spent the night next to a guy, let alone two at once. I hope I don't snore or kick or talk in my sleep.

The sooner I get there, I reassured myself, *the sooner I'll stop worrying.*

But all that accomplished was to make the next hour inch by so slowly, you would've thought someone had poured a bucket of tar over the hands of the clock.

7:35 A.M.: Pull on jean shorts. Cut tags off new mocha-colored tank top.

7:41 A.M.: Unload backpack to make sure I remembered everything. I did. Repack.

7:59 A.M.: Study reflection in mirror. Decide new mocha-colored tank top is too revealing around chest. Change into T-shirt.

8:04 A.M.: Bring Moxie downstairs for quick pee.

8:21 A.M.: Notice that toenail polish is half chipped off. Borrow Mom's nail polish remover and get rid of rest.

8:29 A.M.: Pick up book. Reread same paragraph three times and still have no idea what it says.

8:34 A.M.: Study reflection in mirror. Sigh. Change back into new mocha-colored tank top.

8:35 A.M.: Realize that if I don't instantly evacuate apartment, I might truly go bonkers.

✦ ✦ ✦

Other than a scattering of cigarette butts, there were no signs of life on the roof.

Much better up here, I thought, swallowing a mouthful of cool air, *much more peaceful.*

Just then the door to the stairwell creaked. I glanced over my shoulder, only to spot J.D., a Yankees cap on his head, a baseball mitt in his hand. My knees nearly buckled out from under me. This was just like in my fantasy. *We'd run into each other on the roof one day, start talking, really hit it off. . . .*

"Hey there," he said, flashing a sexy smile.

My pulse started racing. I wondered if I was entering the Danger Zone, which is what my old gym teacher called it when someone's heart rate exceeds 240, putting them at risk of cardiac arrest. Now *that* would be a mess. I tried to picture J.D. hunched over me, administering CPR.

At least you'd get to do mouth-to-mouth, I could imagine Phoebe saying.

Yeah, but I'd be unconscious, I'd tell her, *so it wouldn't really count.*

"Sara, right?"

He asked me that the last time I saw him!

"No . . . it's Sammie."

"Right," J.D. said.

According to my fantasy, by this point we were supposed to be getting below the surface, each listening to what the other had to say, adult to adult.

"I just came up to check the weather." J.D. punched his fist into his mitt. "I'd better motor if I'm going to get to my game on time."

Motor? Who says motor anymore? While we're at it, who *ever* said motor?

J.D. started across the roof. Right before he stepped into the stairwell, he turned and said, "Catch you later, Sara."

As the door slammed shut, I looked out into Central Park. This is the third time he's gotten my name wrong.

J.D. plays baseball, so he knows the rules.

Three strikes and you're out.

Even if you have angular cheekbones and lips that make me want to suck on them all night.

CHAPTER TWENTY

"**B**ad news," Eli said, locking the front door behind us. "Shay just called . . . he can't come."

"Why not?" I set my backpack in the hallway. The apartment was quiet. Shira and Becca must have already left for the day.

"He had an asthma attack last night that landed him in the emergency room."

"Oh, no . . . is he okay?"

"Yeah. This sort of thing happens a few times a year. But his doctor thinks he should stay in town, just in case."

"That's too bad."

"I know. He said to tell you hello."

We stood there for a second looking at each other.

Eli's poison ivy was mostly cleared up, just a few dry patches on his neck and arms. I liked the way he'd pulled his hair back into a ponytail. It showed off his long eyelashes and olive-colored tan. I tried to think of something to say, but my mind was drawing a blank.

"My mom bought some food for us to bring along," Eli said. "Do you want to help me pack it?"

"Sure."

Once we were in the kitchen, I watched Eli dig through the refrigerator. As he loaded a half dozen bagels, four nectarines and some cheddar cheese into a plastic bag, he explained that Max and Ellen were driving in from New Jersey and would ring the buzzer when they arrived. I glanced at the corkboard next to the phone, where I'd once seen that message from Jenna. This time it was empty, except for the colored pushpins that someone had arranged to form a smiley face.

"Do you want one?" Eli was holding up two peaches. I nodded.

"They're really drippy."

As Eli handed me a paper towel, we caught each other's eyes again.

"I like your shirt," he said.

I reached my hand up to my tank top.

"It really brings out the brown in your eyes." Eli spun toward the sink and began filling a bottle with water.

It was only when the buzzer rang a minute or two later that I realized I was still touching the front of my shirt.

I must have done a double take when Max jumped out of the minivan parked on the street, because he grinned as he slid our bags into the back.

"Uncanny, isn't it?" he asked.

"I can't believe it. You look exactly alike."

And I wasn't exaggerating. Eli and Max could have easily passed for brothers, practically twins if they were the same age. They had identical blue eyes and curly, dark hair, except Max wore wire-frame glasses and his eyebrows met in the middle, above his nose.

"Don't mind me for not helping." Ellen skipped down the steps of Eli's building and hopped into the passenger seat, sticking her bare feet out the window. "I'm feeling lazy today."

"You *should* mind her." Max slid the back of the minivan shut. "Ellen's copping attitude again."

"Copping attitude?" Ellen pulled her feet in as Max started the engine. "I'll cop you."

I glanced at Ellen, with her long, black hair twisted

into a messy bun. She was very unique-looking, maybe part Asian or Hawaiian.

As Ellen poked her foot into Max's ribs, he yanked at her toes, reciting "This Little Piggy." Ellen squirmed away, shrieking that she was ticklish. I smiled as we took a right turn. I could already tell I was going to like Max and Ellen.

"You should've seen the traffic coming into the Lincoln Tunnel." Max adjusted his rearview mirror. "It was a mass exodus from New Jersey."

"Is that where you're from?" I asked.

"For now at least," Max said. "Ellen and I are sharing an apartment in New Brunswick, finishing up at Rutgers."

"And living in sin," Ellen chimed in as we started over the George Washington Bridge.

We couldn't have been on the Palisades Parkway for fifteen minutes when Ellen announced that she had to pee.

"*El,*" Max whined, "you just went at Aunt Shira's."

"What does that have to do with anything? When you gotta go you gotta go."

"Ellen has a bladder the size of a pecan," Max explained to Eli and me.

"About the same size as Max's brain," Ellen retorted.

But after a few minutes, Max switched on his signal and turned into a rest area. The car hadn't come to a complete stop when Ellen leaped out the door and peeled toward the bathroom.

We made it to Bear Mountain in a little over an hour, even though Ellen insisted we stop once more along the way. Just before we pulled out of the second gas station, Max turned in his seat so he was facing Eli and me.

"I'm hereby appointing you the Fluid Police," he said. "If either of you catches Ellen near *anything* wet, I give you permission to clamp your hand over her mouth."

"Dream on, Maximilian, dream on," Ellen chided as she popped the cap on a bottle of iced tea and took a long swig.

"Got that?" Max shifted the car out of park and pulled back onto the Palisades.

We all voted to go directly to the mountain rather than setting up our tents at the campground, which was only a short drive away.

"Play now, work later," Max sang as he grabbed Ellen's hand and started across the crowded parking lot.

At first, the trails were congested, but as the ascent

steepened, we passed fewer and fewer people. The hiking was beautiful: clear paths, craggy rocks and lush trees that offered shade from the glaring noontime sun. After an hour or so, we reached a clearing over a cliff, with a spectacular view of the Hudson River in the distance.

"Good place to break, El?" Max asked, pulling up his T-shirt to wipe the sweat off his forehead. I noticed a line of hair running from his belly button down into his shorts.

"Fine by me," Ellen said.

Max passed around a bottle of water as Eli swung his backpack off his shoulders, pulling out a Swiss Army knife and the bag of food. After we'd all grabbed a bagel, Eli sliced off a chunk of cheese, handed it to me and then cut one for himself.

"Are we staying at the same campground as last year?" Eli asked, handing the knife to Max.

"Yeah . . . Beaver Pond or Beaver Creek, or something." Max tossed a wedge of cheese into his mouth. "I hope you brought your swimsuits because there's a lake on the grounds."

Ellen had been quietly munching a cinnamon-raisin bagel, but as soon as Max said *swimsuit,* her head jerked up. "I'm convinced that women's swimsuits were invented by a misogynist."

"El," Max asked, "what are you talking about?"

"Think about it. While guys hit the beach in shorts, women are expected to wear these skintight numbers. When they're not giving you a constant wedgie, they're showing off every bit of cellulite you didn't even know you had. And with all that, you're supposed to parade around in front of people, acting comfortable?"

"Uh-oh," Max said, "I'm afraid Ellen's getting on one of her feminist kicks."

Ellen began to sneeze, little quick ones, three or four in a row.

"Whenever Ellen gets worked up, she begins to sneeze," Max explained to Eli and me.

"*Of course* I'm worked up. You say *feminist* as if it's a dirty word. All feminism means is that women are entitled to the same rights as men . . . so with that definition"—Ellen sneezed two more times—"anyone with half a pecan-brain is a feminist."

"I'm a feminist." Eli rubbed the knife blade on his shorts before snapping it closed.

"Me too," I said, "definitely."

"Your generation"— Ellen cast a glance over at Max, who was devouring a nectarine—"is much more enlightened than mine."

We were all quiet.

"What did I miss?" Max shook his head. "Why is everyone staring at me?"

Ellen leaned over and kissed Max's cheek. "Don't worry, Maximilian, I'll convert you yet."

"What did I miss?" Max asked again as he tossed his nectarine pit over the cliff.

◆　◆　◆

I recently heard this line in a John Lennon song that really hit home. It went something like *Life is what happens to you while you're busy making other plans.* The way I see it, he was saying that we spend so much time fretting about the future that we forget to enjoy the present. I know I'm guilty of doing that. It just seems like there's always so much to worry about.

But today was different. Maybe it was being out in the country, breathing clean air, getting dirty. Or maybe it was spending time with Max and Ellen, which was like watching a live comedy routine. Or maybe it was being around Eli.

Whatever it was, it was turning out to be one of those days where I wasn't even thinking, I was just living. I couldn't believe how smoothly everything was going. That is, until we got to this roadside diner, where we'd stopped off to grab dinner on our way to the campground.

We were sitting in a booth Max and Ellen on one side, Eli and me on the other. Max had ordered a hamburger and potato salad. Ellen, Eli and I were getting grilled cheese with french fries on the side. The waitress had just brought our drinks when Ellen whipped the paper off her straw and looked from Eli to me and back to Eli again.

"So," she said, sipping her Sprite, "how long have you two been together?"

Eli and I froze. The table fell silent. It suddenly seemed like everything was moving in slow motion.

There ain't no doubt in no one's mind that love's the finest thing around, James Taylor sang in the background.

My cheeks felt so hot I thought they were going to catch fire.

After an eternity, Eli finally mumbled, "We're not together," and dove into his Coke.

"I just thought by the way you look at each other . . ." Ellen's voice trailed off.

"El?" Max pushed his glasses up on his nose. "Remember what to do when you're at the bottom of a hole? You've got to stop digging."

As the waitress arrived with our food, Ellen began sneezing, four, five, six rapid sneezes.

Eli and I still hadn't looked at each other.

"I just put my foot in my mouth, didn't I?" Ellen blew her nose into a napkin.

Eli and I still hadn't said anything.

"Ellen's foot"—Max held the Heinz bottle over his hamburger so the ketchup slowly dripped out—"is surgically attached to her mouth."

"You're one to talk!" Ellen grabbed the ketchup out of his hand and poured it over her fries. "We were in line at the grocery store the other day and Max asked this lady when her baby was due and she was like, 'I'm not pregnant.' You put your entire *leg* in your mouth!"

The image of Max with his leg down his throat made me crack up, and as I did, Eli started laughing too. Then Ellen joined in, and soon the three of us were in hysterics.

"She was wearing one of those tent dresses." Max took a bite of his hamburger, smearing ketchup on his cheek. "How was I supposed to know any better?"

✦ ✦ ✦

We didn't arrive at the campground until it was practically dark. Max left the headlights on so Ellen and I could pitch the tents while he and Eli ran off to collect firewood.

By the time we got the campfire going, the air was so cool that I zipped up my navy-blue sweatshirt. As Max and Ellen huddled under a blanket, we sang everything from "Puff the Magic Dragon" to Jewel to "Jingle Bells," which Max suggested after we thought we'd covered every song ever written.

"I know one we can do," Eli said as soon as we'd made it through the gamut of *Christmanukkah* tunes, as Max had deemed them.

"What's that?" Max asked.

"Do you know 'Brown-Eyed Girl'?" Eli asked.

My stomach did a somersault.

"Sure," Max said, launching into an off-key rendition of Van Morrison's classic.

We fudged our way through the beginning verses, until we reached the *sha-la-la-la-la-la-la-la-la-la-la-ti-da* part. That's when I noticed Eli was looking my way.

Goose bumps popped up on my arms and legs.

"You, myyyyyyyy brown-eyed girl," Max howled.

You, my brown-eyed girl, Eli mouthed to me.

I stretched my legs closer to the flames.

And that's when I caught Ellen watching us, raising her right eyebrow in an expression of keen curiosity.

Just after Ellen tossed the last stick on the fire, Max yawned and declared he was hitting the sack.

"For once you can say it and mean it." Ellen laughed as she pulled the rubber band out of her bun, running her fingers through her long hair. "Get it? We really are sleeping in sacks tonight."

As I lay in my sleeping bag, breathing in the musty

scent of the tent, I felt wide awake. Maybe it was the tree root pressing into my back. I flipped over. Maybe it was being so close to Eli, feeling like he could hear my heart beating. I'd gotten a tingly feeling between my legs as Max and Ellen crawled into their tent. *I wonder if they're having sex.* When Ellen and I were unloading the minivan, I'd noticed her unzipping their sleeping bags so they could lie together. And at first I'd heard them laughing softly, but now it was quiet. I flipped over again.

"Sammie?" Eli whispered. "Are you still awake?"

"Yeah."

"I can't fall asleep. . . ."

"Neither can I."

He was quiet for a second. "Do you want to walk over to the lake? The moon looks really bright tonight."

"Okay."

We slid out of our sleeping bags. As Eli unzipped the tent, I slipped my Birkenstocks on over my wool socks and grabbed my sweatshirt. Eli was right about the moon. It was nearly full and lit up the path that led through the campground.

"It's beautiful out here," I said as we climbed up onto a tall rock overlooking the lake. The moon was casting silver reflections across the water.

"I know."

We sat up there for a long time, tossing stones into the lake, chatting about everything from music to school to life in general. At one point, we were talking about how I'd just moved to the city when Eli asked me if it has been a tough summer.

"How did you guess?"

"I know it's very different," Eli said, "but supposedly after my father died, I was a wreck, full of anger . . . even until a few years ago. . . ."

I tossed a stone into the water, remembering that time our families shared a cabin in the Adirondacks.

"My mom is a great person to talk to about things," Eli added, "really strong."

I nodded as I rubbed my hands across my legs.

"Are you cold?" Eli asked.

"A little . . ."

Eli reached over and took my hand, holding it between his to warm it up. We sat like that for a long time, not saying anything, just looking out at the moon, the sky, the ripples in the water.

"Can I tell you something?" Eli asked after a while.

"Sure . . ."

"I've wanted to do this since that time you and your mom came over to dinner. I didn't think you'd ever notice . . . or I'd ever stop being so nervous around you."

Around me? Someone was nervous around me?

"I thought maybe you were with Jenna."

Eli paused for a minute. "We actually did go out for a few weeks last fall, before I realized that she wasn't at all my type. When I broke up with her I promised I'd always be her friend." Eli paused again. "I know Jenna comes on strong, but she's pretty insecure deep down."

"I got the feeling that she hated me."

"No"—Eli squeezed my hand—"it's more that she was threatened by you . . . but that's still no excuse . . . I told her so after you left."

"You did?"

Eli nodded. "Speaking of that, remember what you said that day . . . about being average?"

I groaned. I don't need to be reminded of that. I remember it quite well myself, every time I look in the mirror.

"I don't think you're average at all . . . I think you're beautiful."

We were quiet for a long time, interweaving our fingers, stroking all over each other's hands.

"Can I tell *you* something?" I asked as Eli traced the calluses on the tips of my fingers.

"Sure."

"I'm glad you asked me to come."

"Can I tell *you* something?"

"Sure." I glanced over at Eli.

"So am I."

I began to tremble.

"Your teeth are chattering," Eli said, touching his fingers to my lips.

The next thing I knew, we were pressing our mouths together. Feeling his lips against mine, tender and moist, sent a current through my shoulder blades and down my back. We wrapped our arms around each other and I rested my head on his shoulder. I liked the way he smelled, smoky from the campfire, but clean, like shampoo. When we kissed again, we used our tongues, exploring the insides of each other's mouths. It was wet, but not drippy, nothing like the Big Slobbery Makeout.

I don't know how much time passed, but before I knew it, the moon was gone and the sky was fading to a pale gray. Eli and I held hands as we crept back through the woods and crawled into our tent. As I slid into my sleeping bag, I could still feel Eli's lips on my face and neck. I ran my hands along my breasts, my stomach, pausing between my legs.

I must have fallen asleep because the next thing I knew, the sun was flooding into the tent and Max was singing, "Up and at 'em, kiddies, up and at 'em."

I got a panicky feeling inside, wondering if Eli would regret last night, if he'd pull me aside and tell me it was a huge mistake. Or worse, not say anything at all, just pretend it had never happened.

But before I could get too mired in fear, Eli propped his elbows on the ground and looked down at me. His hair was rumpled and there was a crease running along the side of his face. "Until a few years ago, I always thought people were saying up and *Adam*."

And I knew it was going to be all right.

CHAPTER TWENTY-ONE

I thought I'd be wiped out from staying up most of the night, but after plunging my head into the chilly lake and gobbling one of the glazed doughnuts that Max produced from the minivan, I actually felt good. I have to admit, it was strange to sit next to Eli at the picnic table while Max and Ellen studied the trail map. As I toweled my hair, I wondered if they could guess that something had happened between us last night.

Not that there was anything wrong with them knowing. Eli didn't seem to mind, at least. Several times during the hike, when Max and Ellen were only a few strides ahead, he reached over and grabbed my hand. I think Ellen picked up on it because when we broke for lunch, as Max and Eli disappeared behind some trees, she flashed me a private, big-sisterly sort of smile.

Around three, we all piled into the minivan and Ellen turned onto the Palisades, this time heading south. My calves were sore and I had at least five mosquito bites on each leg. I rested my head against the window. Maybe I'd close my eyes, just for a second. . . .

"Sammie?" Eli gently tapped my arm. "Sammie?"

I sat up quickly, looking around.

"We're on the West Side Highway. Do you want us to drop you off at your place?"

"Yeah . . . that'd be great."

Ellen double-parked in front of my building so I could grab my stuff from the back. I thanked Max and Ellen and gave them both hugs goodbye. When Eli and I hugged, he let his hand linger on my back as he whispered that he'd call me soon.

The super was standing on the sidewalk, watering the marigolds.

"*Hola,*" he said, waving.

"*Hola,*" I said.

As I skipped into the lobby, he called after me, "I can see the resemblance."

I had no idea what he was talking about, but I didn't get a chance to ask him because a woman was already waiting in the elevator, holding the door for me.

But the second I walked into our apartment, it all made sense. It was one of those moments where, even though you can see everything going on, it still takes your mind a few seconds to process what it means. I don't know why, but this is the order of the thoughts that ran through my head:

1. The apartment is cool. Did the super install our air conditioner already?
2. Why didn't Moxie scurry to the door like she usually does?
3. *Hold on!* What is Dad doing sitting at the kitchen table, thumbing through *The New York Times*?

I froze at the entrance to the room, dropping my backpack at my feet.

"Jimmy D.?" I whispered under my breath.

As soon as Dad saw me, he set his reading glasses on the table and stood up. I noticed he'd gotten several new lines around his eyes and his hair had receded further back on his forehead.

"What are you doing here?" I asked. My knees were starting to shake.

"I got your message yesterday morning, when Aunt

Jayne and I returned from our cycling trip. I caught the red-eye and arrived in the city this morning."

"Where's Mom?"

"She took Moxie for a walk in the park. She thought you'd want to be alone with me."

I stood there, speechless, staring at Dad. He crossed the room and wrapped his arms around me. As I breathed in his familiar smell, tears started pouring down my cheeks. It was as if a dam had broken, because once I began crying, I just couldn't stop.

"I'm so sorry," Dad kept repeating, stroking my hair, like when I was little and would wake up from a nightmare calling out his name. "I'm so, so sorry. . . ."

I sobbed and sobbed, soaking the shoulder of Dad's shirt. When I finally began sniffling, Dad ran into the bathroom and returned with a box of Kleenex. As we sat on the futon, I wiped my nose, tossing the crumpled tissues onto the floor.

And that's when Dad began talking. He told me how he'd booked a room at a nearby hotel, for at least a week, but it could be extended. And how much he regrets taking off from Ithaca so quickly, so selfishly. That he was desperate and scared and could hardly see straight. And how sorry he is that he didn't read the writing on the wall all summer. And how, while he knows I'll never forget, he hopes someday I'll be able to forgive.

"I know this has been horrible for you," Dad said. "I wish I had it to do all over again."

"Are you and Mom still separating?"

"We had a long talk this morning. We're going to live apart this year, to see how things go. But after that, I don't think either of us knows."

I glanced at Dad.

"I'm sorry to drag you through all this. Please understand that Mom and I love you deeply . . . and each other. We're just trying to do the right thing."

I glanced into my lap.

"Even at our age," he added, "the right thing sometimes takes a while to figure out."

As I pressed my thumbnail into a mosquito bite on my thigh, it suddenly hit me. I too have to do the right thing.

✦　✦　✦

I practically sprinted to the three-story brownstone. There were six buzzers next to the door. The bottom one was labeled Frank. After taking a deep breath, I pressed it.

"Yes?" Phoebe's voice sounded through the intercom.

I paused.

"Yes?"

"Hey . . . it's Sammie."

"I'll be right down."

Seconds later, Phoebe charged through the front door and threw her arms around me.

"I'm so glad you came," she said as we walked down her stairs. "I was worried about you."

"You were worried about me?" I paused, shifting my weight from one foot to the other. "I thought you never wanted to see me again."

Phoebe shook her head. "That's exactly what I was worried about."

As we started down Columbus, Phoebe explained how last Sunday, after the whole thing with Kitty, they'd received a call from Pittsburgh. Her grandmother had been rushed to the hospital, complaining of chest pain. Before Phoebe knew it, her mom had rented a car and they were driving west.

"I wanted to call you, to let you know I wouldn't be at the dog run all week," Phoebe added, "but do you know how many Davises there are in the phone book?"

"Seven hundred?"

Phoebe grinned. "At least."

"I thought you were angry about Kitty."

"Kitty pissed me off," Phoebe said, "but I didn't hold it against you. The only reason I left is because I sensed my being there was making it worse."

As we stopped at a light, I turned to Phoebe. Tears

were welling up in my eyes again. "I'm sorry I didn't tell you about my parents. It's just that—"

Phoebe put up her hand to stop me. "You don't have to share anything you don't want to. I know you'll tell me when you're ready."

Tears slid down my cheeks.

"When you weren't at the dog run yesterday or today," Phoebe added, "I was worried something had happened with your parents."

"No." I wiped the tears with the back of my hand. "I was hiking with Eli."

As we started across the street, Phoebe looped her arm through mine. I couldn't put my finger on it, but I could swear there was something different about her.

Before I knew it, we were in front of the dog run, even though neither Moxie nor Dogma was with us. Phoebe unlatched the metal gate and ushered me in. Our favorite bench was occupied by two elderly men, most likely the evening crowd. As we sat off to the other side, Phoebe reached into her back pocket and pulled out a photograph.

"I wrote my phone number on the back"—Phoebe handed it to me—"so something like this doesn't happen again."

I glanced at the picture of me taken that day in Central Park, with the Airedale. I don't know if it was the way I was smiling or throwing out my chest as if I didn't have an insecurity in the world, but I kept thinking, *Maybe Eli is right.* I don't know about *beautiful*, but maybe I'm not so average after all.

"Did you scan a photo for Mountainking?" I asked.

Phoebe shook her head.

"Why not?"

"Because I finally realized something."

"What?"

"Mountainking is a German shepherd. And we all know what they do . . ."

I paused. It was starting to get dark out.

"They lead the blind?" I asked, scrunching up my nose.

"Exactly." Phoebe nodded, "And I decided that I'd rather be the world's first ninety-year-old virgin than be blindly led by someone who dumps me with the click of his keyboard."

As streetlights flickered on, it suddenly dawned on me.

"I just realized what's different about you! You're not wearing your knee brace anymore!"

Phoebe nodded. "I had a long talk with my mom on the drive back from Pittsburgh. I told her I never want to touch another tennis racket as long as I live."

"What did she say?"

"That as long as I take up another extracurricular activity, it's okay with her." Phoebe paused. "Wait a second! There's something different about you too."

I grinned.

"Does it have to do with hiking with Eli?"

I was smiling so hard I thought my face would crack.

"Sammie dearest." Phoebe turned toward me, taking both of my hands in hers. "Tell Aunt Phoebe everything."

CHAPTER TWENTY-TWO

When I woke up the next morning, September was in the air. Not that it was chilly exactly, but the humidity had finally lifted, giving way to the kind of air that reminds me of apples and leaves burning and back-to-school shopping.

I hugged my blanket around my shoulders as I thought about my conversation with Dad yesterday. He had invited me to fly back to California with him, to live in Palo Alto for the school year. My mind had immediately raced to Phoebe and Eli and the fact that I'm actually starting to feel at home in New York City. Dad must have read it on my face, because he emphasized that I didn't have to decide right away, that I could change my mind at any time.

As I looked out at the cloudless sky, this old Bob Dylan song ran through my head. The real title is "Love Is Just a Four-Letter Word," but when Dad played it for me a few years ago, I thought it was love *and other* four-letter words. I remember plunging into hysterics at the notion that love could go hand in hand with all the choice profanities my preteen brain could muster up.

I snuggled deeper in my covers. In a strange way, it sort of makes sense. That along with love comes other four-letter words. Like *hate*, obviously. And *loss*. And *gain*. And most important, *grow*.

I've been thinking about growth a lot lately. Thinking about what Mom said, about friendships having their ebbs and flows. I've decided I'm going to e-mail Kitty really soon. I'm not up for any big talks yet, but if Mom and I end up driving to Ithaca, maybe we could just go for a walk or something.

I could hear Mom's key turning in the lock. A second later, Moxie poked her wet nose in my face.

"You're up already?" Mom asked as she hung the leash on the doorknob.

"Now I am." I wriggled away from Moxie.

"It's a beautiful day. Would you like to go out to breakfast before you meet Dad?"

"Sure." I glanced at the clock. Dad and I had agreed to spend the morning together, renting bikes in Central

Park, maybe even coming back to the apartment so I could show him what I'd learned on my guitar.

As Mom closed up the futon, I threw on some clothes and pulled my hair into a ponytail. Just before we headed out, I grabbed my sweatshirt from the closet. Tying it around my waist, I noticed that it smelled like campfire smoke. My stomach flipped over. The last time I'd worn it was at Bear Mountain.

The waiter had just refilled Mom's coffee cup when she stirred in some cream and said, "I don't know how to put this. . . ."

I took a bite of my waffle and glanced at her. I'd been surprised when she'd walked through the door yesterday with a shoulder-length, layered haircut. She'd explained how she was passing by a salon on Saturday when she caught her reflection in the window and before she knew it a woman named Destiny was snipping away.

Destiny thought this style would show off my eyes, Mom had added.

When Mom said that, it suddenly hit me that the circles under her eyes were finally starting to fade.

Mom picked up her coffee cup and set it down again without taking a sip.

"I guess I want to apologize . . . for being such a wreck this summer."

I was about to say *That's okay* when Mom shook her head.

"No, it's not okay . . . but if it's any consolation, I'm going to start seeing a therapist."

"Really?"

Mom nodded. "And Dad and I had a much-needed conversation yesterday morning . . . about money. Not to go into specifics, but we're going to dip into our savings so I can take the year off, enroll in some art classes, reevaluate my teaching career."

"That's great, Mom!"

"I know."

We were quiet for a little bit. After a while, I said, "I'm sorry I yelled at you last week—"

"You don't have to apologize. There was a lot of truth to what you said . . . which is always the hardest thing to hear."

As Mom reached over and touched my arm, I choked up again, for the third time in less than twenty-four hours. Before I know it, I'm going to turn into a regular crier, just like Mom. An Onion Junior.

✦　✦　✦

Mom and I had been back at the apartment for a half hour when Dad rang the buzzer.

"Do you want me to let him up?" Mom called from the hallway.

"No." I slipped into my sneakers. "Tell him I'll come downstairs."

When Mom returned, she sat next to me on the futon.

"Sammie?"

"Yeah?"

"I want you to know that wherever you choose to live next year, I fully support you either way."

"Thanks for saying that," I said as I tied my laces. "Thanks a lot."

As I was riding down in the elevator a few minutes later, I realized something. Whatever decision I make, I'm going to be in the driver's seat. And I still don't even have my learner's permit yet.

About the Author

WHEN CAROLYN MACKLER was seventeen, she fled her homeland of western New York to attend Vassar College, study in Paris, drive cross-country in a car named Egg and live in eleven different apartments, two half-of-houses and one tent. She eventually made her way to New York City to become a writer. Carolyn's articles have appeared in numerous publications, including *Ms.*, *Jump*, the *Los Angeles Times* and *Adiós, Barbie: Young Women Write About Body Image and Identity*. She has spoken on CBS as well as on radio programs, college campuses and panels nationwide. She is currently working on her next novel. E-mail her at *hellocarolyn@mindspring.com* if you want to know what it's about.